Folks in Tombstone don't waste much time on manners...

The piano stopped abruptly. The much younger and much leaner and meaner-looking gent who'd been trying to pick out some tune on it spun around on the piano stool to snap, "You talk too much, Woody!"

Woody, if that was the solitary drinker's name, turned a paler shade of gray as he protested, mildly, "Hell, everyone knows the durned old mines are flooded, Knuckles."

The would-be piano player rose to a full six feet and then some, talking to old Woody but staring at Stringer as he growled, "What happens in Tombstone is Tombstone's own business, and this dude just up and *said* he worked for a damned *newspaper!*"

Stringer stared back just as friendly as he digested that part about him being a dude. The bully by the piano wasn't dressed any more cow than he was. If anything, the rascal was dressed a mite fancier. The Colt .45 he packed low on his left hip was silver mounted. Its position betrayed him as a southpaw. The grips would have been facing forward if he'd been a cross-draw fighter. Stringer was tempted to see if he was a fighter at all . . .

LOU CAMERON

STRINGER

IN TOMBSTONE

CHARTER BOOKS, NEW YORK

STRINGER IN TOMBSTONE

A Charter Book/published by arrangement with
the author

PRINTING HISTORY
Charter edition/July 1988

ISBN: 1-55773-051-2

Charter Books are published by The Berkley Publishing Group,
200 Madison Avenue, New York, New York 10016.
The name "CHARTER" and the "C" logo are trademarks belonging
to Charter Communications, Inc.

PRINTED IN THE UNITED STATES OF AMERICA

10 9 8 7 6 5 4 3 2 1

CHAPTER
ONE

"This reads plain impossible," growled Sam Barca. The crusty old features editor of the *San Francisco Sun* read farther along the ticker tape before demanding, "How in blue blazes could a town in the Arizona desert get wiped out by a flood?"

Across the desk from him Stringer MacKail went on rolling a smoke. Younger and less excitable than Barca, he observed calmly, "I've seen it rain in Arizona, boss. It doesn't happen all that often, but when it does, watch out."

He sealed the straw-colored paper with his tongue and put the cigarette between his lips to light before he added, "On the other hand, this *is* the silly season. Mayhaps the wire service didn't feel we'd want another two-headed calf or a hen that lays square eggs. Do they say

1

just where in Arizona Territory it's been raining so hard of late?"

Sam Barca nodded. "They do. Tombstone Township in Cochise County. They're seldom so precise when they're making up a silly-season filler from whole cloth. What are you working on right now, Stringer?"

A distinctly uncomfortable look crossed MacKail's features as he replied, with some reluctance, "That argument old John Muir is having with the lumber barons about his pet redwood trees. Thought I'd run over to that grove he's trying to save and see what all the fuss is about, if it's all the same with you."

Barca snapped, "It's not. The lumber companies advertise in this paper a lot more than bird-watchers like Muir ever do. There's no news in whether a redwood tree gets cut down or just goes on standing there. But this story about a whole town getting swept away by a desert deluge can't offend any of our subscribers, whether it's true or not. So you'd best run down to Tombstone and check it out."

Stringer groaned in protest. "Sam, you don't *run* down to Tombstone. You have to change trains a lot and it still takes forever. It's a dinky mining camp tucked between the Mule and Dragoon mountains. When you get there, it's nothing much. The mines bottomed out around the turn of the century. Anyone who would still want to live there no doubt *deserves* to be swept away by a flood."

Barca put the snarl of ticker tape aside as he lit a smoke of his own in self-defense, muttering, "You can take a cowboy off his horse, but you can't take the horse out of the cowboy. If you have to roll those hayseed cigarettes, can't you at least buy tobacco less odorous than Bull Durham?"

Then, just as Stringer was beginning to think Sam had forgotten the dumb wire-service item, Barca shook out his match and mused aloud, "I recall a feature I rewrote about some derring-do in a town called Tombstone, one time. Must have been at least twenty years ago. Wasn't Tombstone where that old windbag, Wyatt Earp, shot it out with Curly Bill at some corral?"

Stringer grimaced. "Nobody knows whatever happened to Curly Bill," he replied. "Earp claims to have ended his career, in several odd ways, depending on which version Earp feels like at the moment. Old Wyatt and his latest wife are living right down the coast in L.A. He's selling lots in the Hollywood subdivision and she's trying to get into the nickelodeon game as an actress. I'm sure they'd both be proud to rehash his wild and wooly younger days with me, if that's what you want."

With a scowl, Barca snapped, "That's not what I want. Nobody cares about what might or might not have happened in a rinky-dink desert town twenty years ago. I want you to cover what's going on in Tombstone *now*. Make it interesting, and I'll give you at least a column at space rates."

As Stringer sighed and turned to leave, Barca demanded in exasperation, "Dammit, MacKail, why don't you pack it in and take the front office up on that staff position? You'd make a heap more money and you wouldn't get rained on half as much, you know."

Stringer smiled sheepishly down at the deskbound Barca. "Rain or shine," he told him, "I enjoy working in the field. You're all too right about what a man can make, writing as a free-lance stringer. But what would I do with the extra money, chained to a damned old time clock?"

He left the frosted-glass corner cubicle before Barca could tell him how much fun it was to work locked up in a box. As he made his way through the crowded press room a pretty stenographer, pretending to be the Gibson Girl, dimpled at him and asked if he needed her services. He smiled back but shook his head and ducked around her. A man who messed with she-males where he drew his pay was a man who still had a lot to learn.

It was foggy outside that morning. He didn't need Sam Barca to tell him there was no news in that. He'd gotten used to the Frisco fog, but it hadn't been easy. Although he was a native Californio, he'd grown up on a cattle spread in the higher and drier Mother Lode country, a good eighty miles east of the Frisco Bay. He knew it would be sunny and dry where he was going, cuss all feature editors, so he was planning his wardrobe for the trip to Arizona well before he reached his boardinghouse on Rincon Hill, south of the slot.

As he climbed the stairs he saw that the gal on the second landing had her own sassy views about wardrobe, considering her door was wide open, as usual. The naked lady, smoking tailor-mades in her long ivory holder, worked nights as a nude model at the art school on Russian Hill. Stringer had yet to see a naked lady crossing Market Street, day or night, so he assumed she had to have *some* duds she wore, *sometime*. But he didn't ask as he passed her door. Messing with gals where you ate could be a dumb as messing with 'em where you got paid.

Up in his own smaller room under the slanting mansard roof, Stringer peeled off the dude duds they expected him to wear in the city and proceeded to put on the more comfortable working outfit of the still fairly wide outdoors. He hauled on his denim jeans easy enough. He had to haul harder to get his spurred black Justins on; riding boots that weren't too tight when you put 'em on meant you weren't too serious about riding.

He tucked a lighter blue work shirt's tails into the jeans and donned a denim jacket over it. He tied a black sateen bandana around his tanned throat in lieu of a tie and topped himself off with the battered Roughrider hat he'd brought home from Cuba. He decided to pack his .38 Smith & Wesson double-action in with the yellow slicker and other possibles. He had to sit on the old gladstone bag to lock it—heading into the Arizona desert when it was acting so odd called for more than the usual possibles.

He was braced for caustic comments on his appearance as he passed the gal on the second landing again, but she just blew some violet-scented smoke and a disgusted look his way. He hoped she was starting to give up on him, too. The situation was rough on both of them, if she had any feelings at all.

The depot was only a short walk toward the waterfront. He got aboard one of the frequent S.P. Coasters, bless it, just as it was fixing to roll south. He waited until they were below San Jose, with nobody fighting him for his seat or space on the overhead luggage rack, before he got up and ambled back to the observation car. He didn't want to observe anything. He'd made this same eight-to-ten-hour trip too often to expect unusual scenery, but they had a bar back there as well.

Stringer ordered Steamer beer and found an empty seat near the door to the rear platform. He'd just settled down when a heavier-set gent, a few years older than he, sat down beside him to ask if he wasn't Stuart MacKail of the *Sun*.

"My friends call me Stringer," he answered, sighing. "I know it's sort of lowly. But, when I don't watch out, there's this tendency to shorten Stuart to Stu, and that's a fitter name for cow-camp grub than a former cowhand."

Chuckling, the stranger said, "My folk didn't let me choose my own name, either. I'm Homer Davenport. I'm working free-lance now, too. Some editors just have no sense of humor."

Stringer considered the older newspaperman with new respect. "I know the feeling. I've seen your political cartoons. You're good, as well as funny. I admired that one you drew of Senator Mark Hanna, dressed in a suit of dollar bills. You headed for L.A., Homer?"

"May as well," Davenport grunted. "I just paid a visit to my old hometown, Silverton, Oregon, up the coast. I don't know why. There sure as hell aren't any jobs for us artistic types and, every time I get away for a while, I forget how spiteful small-town folk can be about a local boy who made good."

Stringer nodded his understanding. "I get that every time I go back up to Calaveras County. I suspect that when we're not in town they like to brag on knowing us when. Maybe we'll both wind up as small-town brags."

Davenport said his own hometown was free to name itself after him, for all he cared. He asked Stringer where he was headed and was told, "To another small town that brags about old boys it had little or no use for when they were in town. You ever heard of Tombstone, Arizona?"

Davenport said, "Sure. Silver mining, right?"

With a wave of his hand, Stringer answered, "Once upon a time—back in the seventies a prospector named Ed Schieffelin struck silver in the Dragoon foothills. It was still Apache country and he'd been told the only thing he'd find in such uncouth parts was his own tombstone. So that's what he named his find, the Tombstone Lode."

"Yeah, I recall the rush," Davenport broke in. "It sounded like a great adventure, but my folks wouldn't let me go. Probably just as well. I heard it was one tough little town while it lasted. You say it's still there?"

Stringer explained, "That's what I'm supposed to find out. The wire services report it swept away by a flood. I had it down as a ghost town, too."

Davenport showed he'd been around by agreeing, "Few silver towns last all that long. If Tombstone lasted twenty years that cuss must have struck a vein indeed. When did it bottom out?"

Stringer answered, "Like you said, about twenty years after old Ed Scheiffelin found it. Lord knows what they've been doing there since. But if nobody was still there, we'd have never heard about that flood."

They rode in silence for a time. Then Davenport mused, "It's starting to come back to me. Didn't the notorious Wyatt Earp do wonders and eat cucumbers in Tombstone, years ago?"

"He wasn't notorious back then. But in recent years he's been selling real estate down in Hollywood and the gents who write one-reelers for the nickelodeons have sort of discovered him. Wyatt's been giving 'em pointers on the Wild West and, hell, how are they supposed to know?"

Davenport laughed. "They were showing *The Great Train Robbery* in Portland as I passed through. I thought it was supposed to be a comedy till everybody wound up dead," he said, shaking his head in amused wonder. "Why don't they hire old boys that was there, if they want some tips on making Wild West pictures? Buffalo Bill, Frank James, and even Cole Younger are still around if they want to be authentic."

Stringer shrugged. "Old-timers like Wyatt Earp no doubt work cheaper, whether he was there or not."

Tiring of the subject, they wandered on to other topics of mutual interest to newspapermen, bought each other a few rounds, and then Davenport consulted his watch and announced, "If we don't ease our way up to the dining car before the noonday rush we'll have to stand in line and eat off dirty linen."

Stringer agreed that sounded dreadful, so they headed for the dining car. It was quite a hike, since one was expected to drink at the rear yet eat at the front of the S.P. Coaster. They got there just as a colored waiter was starting to move back the other way with a set of chimes to signal the start of the stampede. He gave Stringer a dubious look. Stringer was glad he had on his bandana; they sure were getting fancy on the S.P. line.

Dressed more properly, Davenport led the way to a table near the far end and the two men sat down. When another waiter came to take their orders Davenport refused to surrender his menu, saying he intended to keep it as proof they actually wanted thirty-five cents for a plate of plain old roast beef. The waiter didn't argue; he was working for tips.

Stringer said he'd have fish, just for the halibut. As the two of them waited for their orders he sipped ice water and watched, bemused, while the cartoonist sketched something or somebody on the back of his menu with quick sure strokes of his pocket Waterman. Stringer could see it developing into the head and shoulders of some cuss. He said, "I'd have worn my suit and tie, had I known I was to be immortalized by the one and original Homer Davenport."

The cartoonist replied in a near-whisper, "I'm not drawing *you*. Don't turn around. There's a mean-eyed rascal, two tables behind you, who's been dogging your tracks since you first came into the club car."

Stringer suggested, "Mayhaps he just likes to drink beer and eat lunch, the same as the rest of us."

But Davenport insisted, "Trust me. I'm a knockaround hairpin with an eye for trouble. I did consider the simple fact that it's a free country, back in the club car. But the jasper's been staring at you, and keeping you in sight, in a manner that would be suggestive of a jilted lover—if either of you looked the type."

He handed the sketch across the table. Stringer murmured, "I'd have never left my .38 packed away if I'd expected anything *this* ugly to be aboard the same train."

Asked if he knew the mutt Davenport had just sketched, Stringer had to think about it. He knew Davenport was good. The notorious cartoon he'd drawn of Mark Hanna had been a perfect likeness, if somewhat vicious, so it was safe to assume that the mysterious gent glaring at his back right now did have eyebrows that met in the middle, and didn't shave his lantern jaw too often. Davenport had sketched his duds less definitely, with just a suggestion of an open shirt under a checked coat or vest. Stringer asked the cartoonist which they were talking about and Davenport said, "Sporty vest, red and green plaid over a dark blue army or work shirt. For Pete's sake, you need more than a *face* like that to go on?"

Stringer replied, "I've never seen the ugly cuss before. Is he wearing a gun rig?"

"Not so far," Davenport answered. "He could be packing a belly gun and, either way, he has that walk."

Stringer didn't ask what kind of a walk. He was a knockaround hairpin, too, and once one became familiar with the tensed-up stride of trouble in motion, further description was academic.

Davenport continued, "There's two of us to one of him, and I just so happen to have a four-shot .32 in my breast pocket."

Just then the waiter brought their orders, so Stringer waited until they could discuss such matters in private before he told his fellow newspaperman, "I heard you Oregon loggers were sort of prone to direct action. I'm a dally roper, myself. I like to play the critter with enough slack to keep us both from looking foolish."

Davenport insisted, "Even as we discuss the son of a bitch he's glaring daggers at your back."

Calmly, Stringer replied, "That, too. If just *looking* dirty counted, I'd no doubt be engaged—or worse—to an artist's model I know back in Frisco."

He swallowed a morsel of halibut steak before he added with a faintly embarrassed grin, "Since you must have gone to art school, there's a question about such studies that I've always been curious about. When you old boys are sitting there, drawing pictures of a stark-ass nude model, does it or does it not give you a hard-on?"

Davenport chuckled wistfully before replying, "It depends on how good-looking they are. We weren't supposed to take models out, and vice versa, but sometimes there was more vice than versa. I can't speak for the female or effeminate students in my class, of course. I only recall both groups blushing more than I did when we had *male* models to sketch. You can sketch a naked lady's welcome mat with just a few side swipes of a Conté crayon, but you have to look harder, and let everyone else *see* you're looking harder, when it comes to rendering the details of male anatomy." Then he said, "Uh-oh, the brute who's been acting so interested in your anatomy is getting up from his table. I never took him for a picky eater on a diet, but, there he goes. I hope he's not planning to ambush you in the gent's room."

He wasn't, it turned out. Just as Stringer and Davenport were deciding on dessert, the train stopped at Soledad and Davenport gasped, "There he goes! On the double!" Stringer turned just in time to see a hulking figure obscured by window grime and steam as it dashed across the platform to vanish into the little depot. Davenport read the sign above the depot door and muttered, "I didn't know this was a regular stop. What do they grow in Soledad?"

Stringer, who rode this line more often, said, "Mostly fruit and truck. I hear there's a prison camp around here, too. You're right about it not being a regular stop. You have to flag the engine if you want to get on, or ask the conductor if you want to get off, in Soledad."

Davenport opined, "He sure must have wanted to get off, and I just can't see him as a farm worker. Maybe he wants to visit some kin?"

Stringer merely said, "That lets *me* off the hook as his main desire. Maybe he was just glarey-eyed by nature."

Davenport thought before he decided, "He was glarey-eyed, all right. He acted more human, back in the club car, until you got on the subject of Tombstone."

Stringer asked, "Weren't we *both* discussing Tombstone?"

Davenport countered, "You were the only one who said you were *going* to Tombstone. I told you, and no doubt him, that I was only riding as far as L.A. I got the distinct impression he didn't like the idea of *anybody* going to Tombstone right now."

The train started up again. Stringer said, "Well, whether I upset him or not with my travel plans, there's nothing he can do about it now."

But Davenport asked, "Want to bet? There's a telegraph office in, or close to, every railroad depot. Western Union can beat you almost anywhere in the country, by hours. If I were in your boots I'd stay well clear of Tombstone until I found out why someone else seems so interested in it."

Stringer said, "I'm a reporter. It's my job to find out if and why things seem suddenly interesting. To tell the truth, all I was expecting to find, once I got there, was a sort of soggy ghost town."

Grimly, Davenport said, "We gave ourselves away as newspapermen, too, before I noticed that glarey-eyed rascal listening in on us. Are you sure you wouldn't rather do a feature about the Wild West two-reelers they're making down in L.A. these days? I know the nickelodeon is likely to be just a passing fad, but what if we throwed in on a comical free-lance article with the text by you and the amusing illustrations by me?"

Stringer said, "I have a better idea. Why don't you come along with me to Tombstone and illustrate whatever could be happening *there* right now?"

Homer Davenport shook his head gravely. "No thanks," he said. "I only like to sketch ghost towns when I know for sure that nobody is *haunting* 'em."

CHAPTER
TWO

Stringer was sorry to part with Homer Davenport when they got to L.A. that afternoon, for the cartoonist was interesting company and Stringer was less than a third of the way to Tombstone. As the S.P. he'd changed to rumbled and rolled its weary way across the greasewood flats to the east, Stringer would have settled for the company of the gal back home on the second landing. He knew the scenery outside would get even duller after sunset, and he'd never learned to sleep soundly sitting up. The damned old timetable made it impractical to stretch out in a Pullman berth, even if he'd felt like spending the money. He knew they wouldn't be folding down the bunks and drawing the canvas hangings in the forward Pullman cars before nine P.M., and he had to change trains again at Tucson before three A.M.

After that, according to the timetable, it got worse. The

spur line serving Tombstone had gone out of service once there was no silver ore to ship, and the best S.P. could offer by rail, now, was the flag stop at Fairbank on the Rio San Pedro. Stringer knew he would have to be awake, well before they got there, if he wanted the conductor to drop him off anywhere *near* Tombstone.

So he had a late light supper in the diner and put off drinking and smoking in the club car by reading through the copy of *Collier's* he'd picked up in the L.A. depot. The latest adventure of Sherlock Holmes was sort of interesting. But Stringer felt old Sea Power Mahan's article calling for Teddy Roosevelt to build an even bigger Great White Fleet was overdoing Manifest Destiny a mite.

That reminded Stringer of his possible need to defend his own national integrity, so, feeling just a touch foolish, he hauled down his gladstone to unpack his gun rig and put it on. By buckling it so the .38 rode higher than usual on his right hip and buttoning his denim jacket over it, he figured the only folk who might notice would most likely know enough about guns not to ask foolish questions of a fellow traveler.

By the time he'd armed himself and finished the magazine it was getting too dark for easy reading, anyway. The overhead Edison bulbs were only forty-watters when they were lit and the S.P. must have thought it saved a heap of money by waiting until the sun outside had set entire before they switched them on.

He took out the menu Davenport had given him and unfolded it for another sober study of that ugly mutt aboard the earlier train. Then he put it back in the same jacket pocket and got up to amble back to the club car.

Nobody half so ugly seemed to be there. Stringer got a

beer at the bar and found a corner table to set it on as he took out the makings and proceeded to roll a smoke as well.

He did so with the full knowledge that the gentle draft through the club car put him downwind of anyone who might be offended by the delicate scent of smoldering Bull Durham. So when a burly gent who'd been seated at another table with a gal in a big hat commenced to loom over him and demand he put out his infernal smoke before he'd even lit it, Stringer smiled up at him, sincerely puzzled, to ask in a less offensive tone, "Is there a No Smoking sign I missed, somewhere about?"

The husky fellow rested his weight on the knuckles of his hamlike fists, planted perilously close to Stringer's beer schooner on the tiny table between them, as he growled, "Sign or no sign, you'd better not light up if you know what's good for you!"

Stringer thought about that as he sealed the paper with the tip of his tongue. He hadn't been smoking in his forward coach seat because he'd noticed ladies riding up yonder, some with little kids. The gal at the next table didn't strike him as a lady, unless red velvet, black lace, and at least two coats of face paint were the newest fashion. The hulk defending her delicate nose was dressed as sporty. There was a diamond stickpin almost big enough to serve as a bicycle headlight flashing from the purple silk tie he had peering over the top of his brocaded maroon vest. His brown derby hat looked new and mighty free of dents, considering what seemed to be wearing it. Stringer put the twist of Bull Durham between his lips, struck a match, took his time lighting it, and then asked, quietly, "Tell me what's good for me."

It was the burly stranger's turn to study some. Anyone could see he had a good forty pounds and likely the reach on the tall but more sinewy Stringer. After that things got less certain. The calmly interested face meeting the bully's usually intimidating glare was clean-cut and unscarred. But it was well tanned by sun and wind and the wide-set amber eyes could stare warm as old gold or icy as cold brass, depending on what they were staring at. Stringer had never liked bullies, even when he'd been small and skinny enough to be afraid of them—which he hadn't been, for some time. There was nothing like growing up in cow country and working your way through college as a cow-hand to put muscle and lightning-fast reflexes on most any-one, and Stringer had been born to a tall and warlike Highland clan to begin with.

The woman at the next table saved the situation by call-ing her escort back, softly but as sharply as if he'd been her dog. That allowed him to nod down at Stringer grimly and mutter, "Later," as he straightened up and moved back to the safety of a woman's skirts. Stringer refrained from blowing a taunting smoke ring after him. He made sure, in fact, that the draft was wafting his smoke through the corner vent on his far side before he relaxed a mite more to enjoy both his smoke and his suds.

He didn't relax all the way, of course. He could see the confrontation hadn't gone unnoticed in the crowded car; often some other asshole would take up the cause, once he had enough under his own skin to feel surly.

This state of affairs made the ride more interesting as they rumbled on through the desert night. But just a beer and a couple of smokes later the garishly dressed couple got up and left. Stringer stared at the clock above the bar wistfully. They hadn't even made it to the Colorado River yet and he'd been sort of counting on the sullen bastard to keep him alert and thus awake.

He perked up again, however, when yet another stranger—also on the tough side—stepped away from the bar, grabbed the empty chair the first bully had just vacated, and swung it about to sit down, uninvited, across from Stringer.

As Stringer's eyes narrowed thoughtfully, the new pest said, "I'm on your side, whoever you may be. For a minute, there, I thought I was going to have to earn my keep, the noisy way, and I just hate noise."

Stringer sized him up for a moment before he said, "I give up. Railroad dick, or on your way to pick up a prisoner?"

The other man, who had a few years on Stringer, chuckled and said, "You was right with the first guess. My job is to see that passengers aboard this line are neither robbed nor shot while still aboard. There are times I wish I'd taken up the violin, like my dear old mother wanted me to. Were you aware, just now, whose face you was blowin' smoke at?"

Stringer shrugged his shoulders. "I did get the impression he must have thought he was somebody tough," he allowed.

The railroad dick said, "He's not distinguished as a thinking man. Lucky for both of us, the lady with him, Faro Fran, spotted me at the bar just in time. Her less sensible escort was the one and original Skagway Sam, a knowed associate of Soapy Smith, up Alaska way."

With a frown, Stringer objected, "Soapy Smith was shot dead some time ago, right?"

The railroad dick shook his head. "Not that long ago," he said, "and Skagway Sam fought his way through them vigilantes. As you just saw, they've given Alaska back to the less dangerous wolves, now that the gold strike up yonder seems to be bottoming out. I wish I knew where they was headed, now. I've always wanted to get in on a gold rush, early enough to matter."

"I was up Alaska way the night they hailed the dawn of this new century," Stringer said, nodding. "My head still hurts to think about it. I got there too late for the really big strikes, too. I don't recall anyone called Skagway Sam at that big New Year's party, although, come to think of it, there were a mess of whores wearing lots of face paint."

"I figured you for a wandering young gent," the railroad dick claimed. "I don't suppose you'd like to show me any I.D. you might see fit to pack along with that gun you got on, eh?"

Smiling, Stringer said, "You're wrong. I've generally found it easier to show my press pass and gun permit than to cause needless anxiety to gents as peace-loving as me."

The older man looked anxious indeed until he saw that Stringer was drawing nothing more lethal than a billfold from under his jacket. As he studied Stringer's credentials he relaxed visibly. "Hell, I know you, son," he exclaimed. "I mean I've read the stuff you write for the *Sun*. Was you serious or working for the Democrats when you sent that piece from Cuba about old Teddy's famous charge up San Juan Hill?"

Stringer put his billfold away with a sigh as he told yet another avid reader why his dispatches from the front during the recent war with Spain had disagreed so often, and so much, with more thrilling eyewitness accounts filed from the cantinas—and worse—of Havana. He finished by pointing out, generously, that some of the other correspondents had no doubt been more worried about yellow jack than Spanish bullets. Hardly anyone on the American side had actually been killed by the enemy, but the fever had put one hell of a mess of good men on both sides in their graves.

"My sister's oldest boy told us much the same tale when he got mustered out of the Roughriders. So I know you ain't a bullshit artist, MacKail. Now I'm going to give you a no-bullshit tip on surviving your quarrel with Skagway Sam."

Stringer cocked an eyebrow. "Oh? I thought it was over, sort of peaceful."

With a disgusted look, the railroad dick said, "Gunslicks like Skagway Sam can't afford to end fights peaceful. You called him and you backed him down, in front of a woman and a whole mess of men. He knows that such stories are sure to get around in time. So he means to nip the story, and you, in the bud."

"You'd best sit somewhere else in that case," Stringer replied indifferently. "You're in my line of fire if he comes back for a rematch, pard."

The older man shook his head, explaining, "Not here, in a car full of witnesses, dammit. This is the twentieth century, not Dodge in the seventies. Cold-blooded murder wasn't as easy to get away with, then, as some would have it, but everyone who rides this line knows the sad story of the Tucson yards. Your best bet would be to get off when this train hits Yuma."

Stringer shook his head stubbornly. "I don't have any business in Yuma. I can't say I know the sad story of the

Tucson yards, either. Is it a good place to lay for someone you don't like?"

The old-timer, who knew the line better, nodded grimly. "It's where you got to change trains, in the dark, with a heap of handy shadows all about as you stumble across a mess of tracks and switch points. The first time the Tucson yards was used so fatal was back in the spring of '82. The victim was Deputy Sheriff Frank Stillwell. He was found dead by the tracks after his killer—or killers—had left aboard any number of trains passing through the junction late at night. They got away clean. The same trick's been used since. That's why I'd get off at Yuma, instead, if I was you."

Stringer said, "Maybe it's just as well you're not me, then. But I thank you for the warning just the same. Wasn't the unfortunate Frank Stillwell one of the gents accused of gunning down Morgan Earp in some pool hall, earlier?"

The railroad dick said, "It wasn't some pool hall, it was Bob Hatch's, in Tombstone. Some said the deed was done by Stillwell. Others said it was Pete Spence or a Mex calt Florentino Cruz. Suffice it to say, Morgan Earp's body was being sent to their family home in California, by way of the Tucson yards, the very night Frank Stillwell wound up just as dead there. What he might have been doing there that night is still pure mystery. It couldn't have been Morgan Earp as shot old Frank. Some say it was Doc Holliday, Sherm McMasters, Turkey Creek Jack, or even one of the other Earp boys. My point is that the deed was never pinned on nobody. That's just the way it goes when you gun a man in the dark before no witnesses. You'd best get off at Yuma."

Stringer sipped some beer as he thought about that.

Then he put down his schooner, firmly, and said, "Skagway Sam might not even know about that natural ambush point down this line. Thanks to you, I do. It's not all that easy to ambush an armed man when he's on the prod and expecting you to try. If Skagway Sam's half as good as you say, he'll know that, too. He's traveling with a woman and Lord knows how much other baggage. They must be heading somewhere farther east than Tucson, so they'll have their own train connections to worry about. I'd look dumb as hell getting off at Yuma just because I was spooked by the dark."

Heaving a sigh, the older man said, "Maybe so. But either way, you'd be alive when you finally got where you're going." Then he asked, "Where would that be, by the way—El Paso?"

Stringer shook his head. "Tombstone, and please don't tell me I can't get there from here. I know I have to get off at Fairbank and hire a horse and saddle."

"Hell, it's a waste of time, talking sense to lunatics," the railroad dick said, grimacing. "You say you're in a *hurry* to get to Tombstone? There's nothing *there* no more. I hope you didn't tell Skagway Sam you was headed for Tombstone. Catching you all alone, on the desert, has laying for you in the Tucson yards beat all hollow!"

It was hard to stay awake all the way to Tucson, but Stringer had no other choice. The crisp, cool air slapped him wider awake when he stepped out on the observation platform as soon as he felt the train slowing down. Setting his gladstone down, he let his gun rig's buckle out a couple of notches. Then, with gladstone once more in his left hand and his .38 riding lower on his right hip, he prepared to detrain in a less usual manner. He assumed anyone out to do him dirty would be expecting him to get off up forward, with the help of the train crew. There were few stops with platforms along the S.P. line, so the trainmen swung trapdoors up out of the way to expose four steps leading down to just above the level of the tracks and then they provided yellow steel boxes to serve as bottom steps to the grit.

As the train hissed to a stop in the darkness, Stringer forked a long leg over the side of the observation platform, steadied himself with his gun hand, and just dropped to the crunchy railroad ballast. Up ahead, he heard the clatter and clangs of the train crew making things easier for the other passengers getting off in the regulation fashion here.

Stringer had the layout of the Tucson yards pictured in his mind's eye as a sort of Y with the top branches to the east in order to let rolling stock move on to the north or more to the south in that easterly direction. Now that he was there, things looked less simple in the tricky light. He felt sure there was more light on the subject now, thanks to Thomas Edison, than there'd have been the night Deputy Stillwell had met his mysterious demise somewhere around here. Electric lights on strategic but widely spaced poles cast confusing, piss-poor imitation moonbeams as well as long inky shadows in every direction. Up ahead, blurred figures were departing from the right side of the train. Stringer had determined that the passenger train they were supposed to transfer to would be a track or so over in that direction, but a line of empty freight cars, zebra striped in light and shadow, had been left to block the next siding over. The other transferring passengers were hurrying up the slot between the train they'd just left and the awkwardly parked boxcars. Stringer didn't need to be told by anyone that the deal was to move on up and over to passenger cars waiting a siding farther away than they'd have been if *he* was running this dumb railroad.

He started walking faster to catch up with the rest of the crowd. As the couple at the tail end passed through a shaft of light he caught a flash of big hat and red skirt. That made him drop back a few paces, even as it reassured him some; Skagway Sam and Faro Fran seemed more intent on changing trains than on a resumption of hostilities.

He still wanted to let them board well ahead of him, so that he could climb on somewhere else. They were probably traveling fancy, in one of the forward Pullman cars. Stringer know he'd be, if he was traveling with a gal built like Faro Fran. After all, what were a few coats of paint between friends in the cozy darkness of a Pullman berth? She probably smelled swell, too.

Then, just as the shady couple ahead of him were moved through a puddle of lamplight, a darker figure stepped out from between two boxcars, its back to Stringer and the two guns in its hands trained on Faro Fran and Skagway Sam.

Without taking time to think, Stringer drew his own gun with a shout of "No!" The next few seconds got confusing as all hell.

The shadowy gunslick spun on one heel to throw down on Stringer, who naturally fired first. Then Skagway Sam put a round in the poor brute from the other side, which spun him around again and sort of corkscrewed him into the ground. By the time he got all the way down, both Stringer and Skagway Sam had taken cover between widely spaced but solid boxcars. As he stared their way through the haze of gunsmoke, Stringer was not at all surprised to see Faro Fran had vanished from sight for the moment. Stringer called out, "Skagway?" and got no answer.

He heard running footsteps behind him. One of the yard bulls coming his way was toting a bull's-eye lantern. Stringer put his still-warm six-gun away and stepped out into view, hands polite, to call, "Over here. Some bozo just tried to gun a woman in her back! That's him, yonder. Be careful. He was waving at least two guns about, just now."

The two yard bulls stopped closer to Stringer. The one with the bull's-eye trained its beam on him, thoughtfully, then swung it on the body just up the slot. Now that he could see what he'd shot it out with, Stringer saw he seemed to be a middle-aged Mex or breed, wearing a dark charro outfit and a puzzled smile, as if he found it mildly amusing to be dead. The yard bull with the lantern noted the open eyes with six-guns safely scattered on the railroad ballast before he whistled softly and said, "This old boy won't ever back-shoot no more ladies. Where might this lady he was messing with be, right now?"

Stringer said, "They probably ran on to that other train. I have to catch it, too."

The two yard bulls exchanged wary glances. Then the one who was packing a sawed-off shotgun instead of a lantern said, soberly, "Not hardly, mister. You just gunned a man on Southern Pacific property. There'll always be another train for you to catch, when and if Tucson says it's all right for you to move on. Right now we'd best go have us a talk with the law."

He sounded like he meant it, and Stringer couldn't really blame him. He shot a weary look at the man he'd just killed, halfway at least and said, "I think we'd better.

For openers, I'd sort of like to know who he might have been. You see, I'm a newspaperman."

They seemed relieved that Stringer didn't argue. Neither made any unkind suggestions about his gun as the three of them headed back down the slot. Before they got to where he'd gotten off, the eastbound he'd come this far aboard began to roll out of their way. A distant toot told Stringer the train he was supposed to be aboard right now was leaving, too.

The yard bulls swung him north toward a cluster of buildings shaded by a coal tipple over that way. As they cut across the intervening tracks in the tricky light a trio of other men with bigger hats came to meet them. When one called out a wary question about the gunshots, the yard bull with the lantern shone it on Stringer and replied, cheerfully enough, "This gent just shot it out with a Mex, Marshal. Guess who won."

The three Tucson lawmen were less casual about suspects packing guns on their hips. One drew to cover Stringer while a sidekick gently but firmly disarmed him and patted him down for anything else as serious. When he said, "He's clean, Marty," the one with his gun out put it back in its holster and said, "Well, first things usually coming first, we'd best all go have a look at the loser. Do you have a name, you winning cuss?"

Stringer identified himself and offered to show them his papers as they all moved back to the scene of the shooting. With the passenger train no longer blocking the yard lighting, the scene was a lot easier to take in at at a glance. One of the Tucson lawmen dropped to one knee, felt the downed man's throat, and decided, "This one ain't about to answer no questions. Shine that bull's-eye over this way, will you, Smitty?"

The yard bull did. The lawman kneeling by the body rolled it back and forth by one shoulder before announcing, "Hit both ways. Just above the heart from the front and lower in the back from behind. When you shoot an old boy you don't mess around, do you, McKail?"

Stringer said, "I only shot him once. One of the other passengers I was with put that round in his back."

The lawman standing by Stringer, who seemed to be in charge along with Marty, observed, "I hate to appear dubious, MacKail. I feel sure you wouldn't dream of fibbing to the law. But just where might this other helpful gent, who back-shot this one, be right now?"

Stringer said, "Most likely aboard that southbound train that just left. All of us were rushing to board her when that cuss on the ground threw down on the man and woman just ahead of me."

"Right. Maidens in distress are usually ungrateful as all get-out," Marty declared with a hint of sarcasm. "You saved 'em both from this desperado and so they naturally just went on about their own beeswax, leaving you to tidy up after 'em."

Stringer said, "I know it sounds sort of unusual. But they were an unusual couple. I don't know their real names, but if it's any help, he was called Sam and she was called Fran."

Marty said, "Oh, that's a big help, McKail. You know what it looks like, from where I'm standing? It looks like you shot this old boy in the back, for whatever reason, and then finished him off as he spun around, going for his own hardware."

Stringer protested, "You're talking *loco en la cabeza,* no offense. All you have to do is dig the slugs out of him and you can say you're sorry when you see a round from my gun took him in the chest and a round from some other gun hit him from behind."

Old Marty looked disgusted. "Do I look like that Sherlock Holmes or any other such sissy nitpicker to you, MacKail? My own good eyes and ears is all I needs to put this here picture together. Anyone can see he was hit first in the back. The front shot was more fatal. You back-shot him. He spun around to face you, slapping leather, and you done better with your second shot. If you got a lick of sense you won't try to shit the judge and jury with made-up witnesses that just ain't here!"

Stringer started to protest again, then decided he'd better save his breath for his lawyer—a good one—if the *Sun* would spring for the court costs he seemed to be facing.

Then a distant feminine voice called out, "Oh, sirs, sirs, could any of you tell me where to find Deputy Marshal Martin?"

They all turned to face the dark feminine figure making its way uncertainly toward them across the tracks in the tricky light.

Marty said, "You have found me, ma'am. Be caresome of your delicate ankles out here in the yards. What can I do for you?"

As she joined them they could see she was a mousy but not altogether bad-looking little thing with a straw boater pinned atop her dark upswept hair. She said, "They told me at the dispatcher's office that you might be out here and, oh, is that poor man still lying there? Don't you think you should get him a doctor?"

Marty said, "No, ma'am. But is it safe to assume you already knowed he was layed out, here?"

She replied in a scared small voice, "I saw it. It was just awful. He was shooting at a lady in a red dress and then two other men shot him instead! Is the lady all right?"

Marty turned to stare at Stringer as he told the young woman, "She must be. She ain't here. Do you see anyone else, here, who might have been involved in that shoot-out, ma'am?"

The girl looked about uncertainly at first. Then she pointed at Stringer and said, "Oh, dear, I don't want to cause anyone any trouble, but I have to say this young man was the one who shouted a warning and, well, after that they *both* seemed to be shooting at that poor man on the ground."

Marty sighed. "You ain't got nobody in trouble, ma'am," he said. "We're going to want sworn depositions from the both of you before either of you will be leaving Tucson. But you coming forward as a witness may have saved young MacKail, here, a great deal of trouble indeed."

He turned to his junior deputies to add, "You boys had best stay here till the morgue crew arrives. I'll carry McKail and his witness over to the office and we'll see what the coroner will have to say about all this in the morning."

As the three of them headed for the lights across the yard the lawman gallantly took the girl's arm, saying, "Watch your step, ma'am. By the way, do you have a name? They're sure to want me to write it down in my officious report."

She said her name was Matilda Gower, that her friends

called her Tillie, and that she was a librarian who'd been on her way to Tombstone in answer to a help-wanted notice.

Both men were surprised at this, but it was Marty who told her, "I didn't know they still had a library in Tombstone, Miss Tillie. Last I heard, the silver was gone and the town was dead."

She sounded sure enough when she answered, brightly, "It must have come back to life, then. There were lots of other job offerings in the same paper, a heap of them in Tombstone. So *something* must be going on there, now, right?"

CHAPTER
THREE

By the time the Tucson coroner's office opened after nine the two of them had been up all night and then some. Stringer was half-awake on a bench at police headquarters. Tillie had dozed off with her head on his shoulder. By the cruel morning light he could see she was a mite older than he'd taken her for in the soft illumination of forty-watt bulbs. She was still a pretty little gal, but time was starting to pass her by. If she didn't hook a man at her next library she was doomed to middle-aged spinsterhood sure as hell. She had to be at least thirty. She'd confessed just before passing out on his shoulder that her impulse to try a new start in Tombstone had been occasioned by a spat with an L.A. gent who'd been taking out books, and sometimes her, for many a year without establishing his exact intentions. It was funny how strangers meeting up as fellow

31

travelers got to swapping stories about themselves that they'd never tell their neighbors back home.

Stringer opened his eyes hopefully to the sound of boot heels. It was old Marty. He looked like hell in daylight, too. Unshaven and bleary-eyed, Marty cleared his throat awkwardly and sat down on Stringer's far side to admit, "We just got some sort of interesting answers to the all-points we sent out on that Mex cuss you shot it out with. He answers to the description of one Jesus Garcia—funny name for such a sinsome cuss. He's wanted in more places for more misdeeds than you can shake a stick at."

Stringer yawned, asking, "Who gets such bounty money as there might have been posted on such a wayward youth?"

Martly looked away to mutter, "That's something we'd best talk over, studious. You know how Indian-giving some outfits can get, once they see a gent they wanted, desperate, dead or alive, is just dead and in no position to annoy them further."

Stringer asked, "And how were you and the boys figuring on saving me such disappointment?"

Marty tried to sound sincerely helpful as he explained, "If you just can't stand not being knowed as the man who finally caught up with Jesus, you'll no doubt want to hang around here in Tucson until the coroner's jury settles the matter in, oh, say a week or so."

"I'd just as soon be on my way, no offense," Stringer replied, grimacing. "What if we just forgot my part in bringing the owl-hoot to justice? You boys would be as willing to take any blame, or credit, involved, right?"

Marty slapped Stringer's knee with a relieved laugh. "There you go, MacKail. We figured you for a good sport and, like I said, there may not be all that much posted on Sweet Jesus to begin with."

"Are we free to go, then?" Stringer asked.

"Sure," Marty declared. "We got nothing at all on the *gal*. She wouldn't be able to put in on any bounty money if she wanted to. She never turned the rascal in. She just saw you shoot him."

With that, Marty handed Stringer's gun to him and got back up to leave the two of them the chore of whatever came next. Stringer woke Tillie, gently, and as she stretched and yawned like a kitten he told her, "It's over. The two of us are free to go."

"I'm hungry," she replied, in a little-girl voice.

He got her to her feet and picked up his gladstone, saying, "We're in the center of town. There must be some place around here where we can get breakfast. Where's your baggage, by the way?"

She blinked down at the floor, gave a mournful little gasp, and cried, "Oh, heavens, my carpetbag and hatbox were aboard that train that left without us last night!"

"Don't worry. You did tell the conductor you were getting off at Fairbank, right?"

Almost sobbing, she wailed, "No! I told him I was on my way to Tombstone!"

He took her arm in his free hand to reassure her, "Same difference. He'll have dropped your baggage off at Fairbank to wait for you by now. Let's worry about one thing at a time, starting with breakfast."

But as he led her out into the blinding Arizona sunlight, Tillie protested, "Wait, I just remembered my *money* was in a purse in my hatbox!"

Stringer sighed in exasperation. "You sure must not

travel much. Why did you put yourself and all your stuff aboard that other train before you rode to my rescue, for Pete's sake?"

She looked away as she admitted, "I wasn't going to. It was none of my business and, anyway, I expected those people you saved to stand by you. Then I saw them on the train, laughing as if they thought something funny had happened and . . . well, the next thing I knew I was telling the conductor and he said there was nothing he could do about it and I'd have to report it to the dispatcher across all those tracks and then—"

"Don't worry about buying your own breakfast," Stringer cut in, adding, "it's the least I can do. If you left your ticket stub aboard with your other stuff, I'll see that you still get to Tombstone. For openers I have to get you to Fairbank, and then I guess we get to hire a rig."

All the way to the beanery they found down the way to the depot, she kept protesting that she couldn't let him *support* her, as she put it. Once she had some ham and eggs in front of her she dove in as if she hadn't been supported in some time. He was more tired than hungry, so as he ate, slower, he got out his railroad timetable to see how much time they had to worry about. When he muttered, "Oh, suffering snakes!" she asked what was wrong. He told her, "The Southern Pacific. *You* may have heard there's a boom down the line, but *they* sure haven't. The very next train that will drop us off anywhere near Tombstone leaves later this evening, after sundown."

She sobbed, "Oh, Lord, I can't stay up that much longer!"

He replied, "We'll have to check in some hotel and leave a sunset call with the desk. I don't know how much sleep you've had in the past twenty-four hours, but I've had none at all and I was up late the night before."

She toyed with the last of her breakfast toast in awkward silence for a time before she murmured, "Won't we have to tell them we're married if we take a room together, sir?"

He started to explain he'd meant to book separate rooms for the two of them. Then he wondered why anyone would want to say a dumb thing like that. Instead he told her, "You don't have to say anything. I'll sign in for both of us, see?"

She started to shake her head, then smothered a yawn and replied, demurely, "I'm going to fall on my face if we don't do something. But I hope you understand I don't make a habit of going to bed with strange men, sir."

He said, "I'm not all that strange, and you might as well start calling me 'Stuart,' Tillie. You'd sound sort of dumb calling me 'sir' while I was checking us through a hotel lobby."

She didn't call him "sir" or anything else, as it turned out. She just stood red-faced at a magazine rack while Stringer booked them a room and bath at the inexpensive but fairly clean hotel across from the Tucson depot. By the time he had her upstairs, she was sobbing softly. He didn't know how to cheer her up, so he didn't try. As he unlocked the door of their corner room she stared at the one brass bed, gulped, and told him, "You'd better go into the bath while I get undressed for bed, Stuart. It's broad daylight, I left my nightgown aboard that horrid train, and—oh, dear —I hardly *know* you!"

He put down his gladstone, moved into the adjoining bath, and ran the water so he could use the commode discreetly. He was beginning to wonder if she wanted him to sleep in the tub when at last he heard her calling, shyly, "Oh, Stuart? You can come out, now."

When he did he found that she'd pulled down all the shades. It was still light enough to see just her big doe eyes staring timidly up at him from under the top sheet. Her duds were folded neatly over the foot of the bed, her perky straw boater hung on a bedpost. He hung his own hat and gun rig on another. Then he sat on the bed with his back to her and said, "No peeking, now," as he hauled his own boots and duds off.

He was so bone weary as he rolled under the covers with her that he felt sure he could sleep platonic with a strange gal if she really wanted him to. But as she snuggled her naked body up against his and pleaded, "Please be gentle with me, sir," he decided that might be considered rude and, for some reason, he didn't feel half as tired, now.

Even so, as he took her in his arms for some kissing and feeling-up, she sobbed, "Oh, Stuart, I'm so embarrassed and I feel so low down!"

He murmured, "We don't really have to, if you don't want to, Tillie."

She giggled. "Liar. You know what we both want. But how, oh how, shall I ever face you again? You must surely take me for a woman of no shame at all."

He chuckled, kissed her, and assured her they'd done nothing to be ashamed of—yet. Then he rolled her on her back and she welcomed him aboard like an old friend. But, being a librarian, she must have felt duty bound to sob, "Oh, oh, what are you *doing* to me!" even as she proceeded to do it back to him with a skill he doubted she could have picked up from any books, even dirty ones.

She climaxed ahead of him. He was so tired he'd have had some trouble getting there at all if she hadn't been so great in bed. When he came at last and lay panting atop her soft and surprisingly pneumatic body, she murmured, "Well, I was looking for thrills and adventure when I left that drab old library back in Los Angeles, but I hardly expected to wind up a *whore!*"

He kissed her, sleepy-eyed, and muttered, "Don't talk dumb. You know you're just sort of friendly, Tillie."

She shook her head, insisting, "There's no nicer way to put it. I just gave myself to a man in exchange for money. Money he's been spending on me, at any rate. It's the same thing, when you get right down to it."

He was aware he might be getting too heavy for her now, so he rolled off and snuggled her against his side with a soothing pat on her bare shoulder. "It's not the same," he declared. "To your way of thinking, all the married women in this country must be whores, unless they have jobs of their own. It's just natural for us men to pay as we wander through life with you sweet little things. Can we get some sleep, now?"

She must have been feeling refreshed. "What if I'd been the one who paid for breakfast, this room, and Lord only knows what else by the time we get to Tombstone?" she argued.

"I wouldn't have let you. I'm not a pimp. You're not a whore. We're just sleepy pals, I hope," he said through a yawn.

But he hoped in vain. She rolled atop him, kissing him fondly before she announced, "If you mean that, I guess I don't feel so dirty after all."

Then he asked what she called what she was doing as

she began to wake him up some more indeed. He laughed, demanding she let him mount her again to finish right, but she wanted to be the one on top this time; so it was even easier for him as she bounced over him, insisting she didn't know what could have gotten into her as she took as much of it into her as she could manage.

After they'd both climaxed again, she seemed more content just to snuggle against him, crooning, "I guess you'd like to know how I lost my virginity and became so wicked, right?"

Stringer merely yawned again and said, "Not really. Let's save some secrets for that train ride tonight, honey."

He never knew whether she answered or not. He didn't realize he was asleep until the bedside telephone woke him up. As he lifted the receiver, he saw the drawn shades were painted orange by the setting sun outside. He growled, "Yeah?"

In response to this the disgustingly chipper gal downstairs said, "It's almost sunset, Mr. Barca. You said to awaken you about this time, remember?"

Stringer thanked her and hung up. Patting the mattress beside him, he groaned, "Time to rise and shine, little darling."

That's when he noticed he was alone in bed. He rubbed a hand across his sleep-gummed eyes and rolled out to pad over to the bathroom door. He knocked on it and called out, less gruffly, "We've just time to grab a bite before we have to catch that local, Tillie."

There was no answer, so he opened the door. She wasn't in there either. He took a leak, splashed some tap water over himself, and moved back to the bed, muttering, "What the hell?" Suddenly he snapped wide awake and dove for his duds. But when he hauled out his billfold he saw she hadn't rolled him after all. So he got out the makings, fixed himself a smoke, and lit it as he pondered the mysterious ways of womankind.

Unless she'd been lying, Tillie had neither the railroad ticket she'd lost nor the funds to purchase another with. So where in the hell could she be?

By the time he'd smoked his tobacco down Stringer felt tempted just to get dressed and be on his way. He'd *told* the fool gal the train they had to catch would be leaving any time now. If she'd wandered off on her own . . . she'd wind up stranded here if he was gone when she got back.

He punched a pillow back in shape, growling, "We're going to miss that train, sure as hell."

But as he lay back down, much less tired than before, he was surprised to discover he was yawning. "Oh, well," he decided, "a good night's sleep in such pleasant company can't kill you and there's always another train."

But the next time he woke up, he was still alone in bed. He rolled over, went back to sleep, and the next thing he knew a damned old bird was chirping just outside the window and it was starting to get light again. He propped himself up on one elbow, regarded the empty side of the bed beside him with a bemused smile, and said, "All right, Tillie. I can go along with a lady having some second thoughts in the cold gray dawn as well as most men. But this is getting just silly. If you're not hiding under the bed, you'd best come out from wherever you might be. For I mean to board the morning train to Fairbank, come hell, high water, or tears of recrimination!"

•   •   •

His train left a little before ten A.M. Stringer got on alone. Although he'd waited at the hotel and then scouted all about it for the mighty mysterious librarian, Tillie Gower seemed to be just plain gone.

He was still feeling guilty about going on alone as his coach rolled southeast. He knew he'd have felt just as dumb, or more so, waiting back in Tucson for a gal who'd obviously given him the slip. It was why she'd done it that worried him. He hated the thought of a pretty—if feeble-minded—lady wandering about Arizona with just a straw boater to her name. Nothing at all sensible worked. He'd been stood up by gals, same as the next fellow, but he couldn't recall one giving him the slip after things had gotten *that* friendly. It was true a false-hearted woman could act friendly as that when she was out to take advantage of some poor brute. But Tillie had come to his aid, free, and hadn't even run off with his tobacco.

As some redwings perched on a trackside wire caught Stringer's eye, he decided, "Western Union. She found herself in a sticky situation and decided to slip out and wire home for money. That's the only thing that I can figure, even if it does seem sort of insulting."

He began to roll himself a smoke, muttering in a wistful tone, "Ain't that just like a woman? Once they've had their wicked way with us innocent young things they can't wait to drop us and move on to some new conquest."

He was only half-joking. He knew there were such adventurous she-males. They were said to suffer a disorder known to medical science as nymphomania. That was what the docs called it, all right. He was glad *he*-males couldn't catch anything like that. The same docs called a man who ran about screwing one gal after another a healthy specimen. It didn't seem half as disorderly when boys was just boys. Everybody knew girls weren't supposed to be just girls.

Stringer put the peculiar librarian out of his mind for the moment to concentrate on the passing scenery. It was just as well he was approaching Tombstone in broad daylight. He'd been picturing this corner of Arizona Territory all wrong in the darkness, the night before last.

The rolling range outside was higher than the cactus country along the Gila and Salt rivers. There was still a tall green saguaro standing with its hands up, here and there, but he saw much more chaparral, a lot of it mesquite. They got more rain down this way, but the range was badly managed as well as overgrazed. Letting mesquite crowd out your short grass was the mark of a lazy cattle man. Cows could live in mesquite chaparral, if you didn't mind hunting for 'em aboard a giraffe at roundup time.

From time to time he spotted a lone longhorn, wild as a deer, crashing through the chaparral because it had been spooked by the train. In country like this the cowcatcher in front of the locomotive wheels wasn't there for show.

Stringer was just getting good and bored of chaparral when the tracks reached the Rio San Pedro and swung south along its west bank. The boulders and sun-silvered driftwood baking on the sandbars of the broad braided stream told silent tales of horrendous flash floods in the past. But at the moment there was barely enough water to qualify the San Pedro as a creek. When the conductor passed through to announce the next stop, Stringer asked him if the river, yonder, had done any damage to railroad property in the recent flood. The conductor shook his head.

"We laid the tracks above the high-water mark. And I can't say as I recall *any* flooding, all that *recent.*"

Stringer insisted, "I heard Tombstone was just about wiped out by a gully washer, recent as hell. I reckon the valley it sits in has to drain somewhere else, eh?"

The conductor frowned thoughtfully before he replied, "Nope. Tombstone's only ten or twelve miles from the San Pedro, in the same watershed. Someone must have been greening you, son. If anything, it's been drier than usual this year, so far. Just don't go camping on the bottom of no wash, in case your informant was a mite premature."

Then he ambled on down the aisle, leaving Stringer no more enlightened than before. He knew the wire services relayed many a hoax. Their job was to pass on news tips and let any editor really interested follow up on the same. But if someone had been having fun with the newspaper game, the intended humor was just too obscure for Stringer to grasp.

He still got off when the train crossed the river on a timber trestle and stopped at Fairbank, a cluster of frame shacks and 'dobes clustered around a water tower and apparently suffering from the delusion it was a town. There was no depot, you just dropped down to bare gravel. But after he'd done so, Stringer noticed an office shed at the base of the water tower and toted his bag over that way. When he knocked on the door there was no answer. Then an older, red-faced man in bib overalls and a railroader's cap finished waving bye-bye to the departing train and limped over to ask Stringer what he wanted.

Stringer explained, "A young lady named Matilda Gower had some baggage she was hoping they'd drop off here with you. I don't suppose you'd know if she ever picked it up?"

With a slow shake of his head the old-timer said, "Not hardly. I'd recall such a·rare occurrence. Folk are supposed to carry their own stuff on and off, here. We don't mind if freight sets alongside the tracks until somebody comes for it, but we don't hold ourselves at all responsible."

Stringer tried, "What if the train crew just left her stuff by the tracks, then? She had—let's see—a hatbox and a carpetbag?"

The old-timer shook his head again, saying, "Nope. I'd have noticed a hatbox. If I hadn't, the night man would have told me about it when I came on. You never seen such an old biddy hen for gossip. The S.P. rules say we're supposed to pass on any unusual happenings we notice on our own shift. But, I ask you, do you think a couple of Mex kids screwing under the trestle constitutes vital interest to the running of a railroad?"

Stringer agreed that what folk did under a railroad trestle was no doubt their own business. "I was sent here by the *San Francisco Sun* to cover the famous flash flood they just had in Tombstone. You'd have noticed if there's been one, right?"

The older man looked sincerely confused as he replied, "I sure would. Only it's been so dry we're more worried about brush fires than floods around here. Who told you there's been a flood in these parts, son?"

Stringer sighed "A joker with a mighty dumb sense of humor, I reckon. Is there a telegraph station here in Fairbank, pard?"

"I got my own set, inside," the old-timer answered. "But that's only for railroad business. I think they used to have a Western Union over to Tombstone. Can't say if it's still in business. Things have been slow in Tombstone since the mines closed down."

Stringer swore softly under his breath. Then he said, "Oh, well, I may as well be able to say I saw the place, still standing, before I head home. How would I go about getting there from here, pard?"

The old-timer took out a red bandana to wipe his red face as he pondered. After a moment he said, "You could walk it in three or more hours, I reckon. But if I was you I'd hire me a livery mount and just ride over. Hiram Booth, down to the other end of town, has ponies for hire at two bits a day."

Stringer allowed that sure beat walking, thanked the old-timer for the information, and headed for the far end of town, which in truth wasn't all that far anyway.

It was going on high noon. Hiram Booth, who was even older than the geezer at the station, answered his screen door in his long johns and with the observation that it was, dammit, siesta time. But he brightened when Stringer bet him a silver dollar that he couldn't provide him with a decent mount and solid saddle for a day or so. The old man came out in his bare feet and underwear to cackle, "You lose, pilgrim. Follow me and I'll show you stock that could clean up at the Kentucky Derby if I wasn't so merciful."

Stringer followed him back between the 'dobe house and frame stable, where a dozen odd scrub ponies stood listlessly in the shade of some desert willow watered by the overflow of a long, leaky trough. Their owner asked whether Stringer was aiming to ride brushpopping or sedate. When Stringer said he just needed something to carry

him to Tombstone and back, the old man shot him a keen
look and said, "Well, it was you as offered to pay handsome. So I'll put you aboard old Blue Ribbon, that chestnut with the white blaze, there. She'll carry you just about
anywhere you want to go and I'll saddle her decent for you
as well. I got a Vadalia center-fire in the tack room with the
stirrups already let out long. Come one, let's get the gear."

Stringer followed Booth into the tack room at one end
of the stable. The old man took down a harness and throw-
rope from one wall. He handed the rope to Stringer, saying, "I'll tote bridle and saddle out. You rope old Blue
Ribbon. I ain't about to step in no corral in my bare feet."

Stringer chuckled, preceded the old man back out to the
corral, and shook out a loop before opening the gate. As he
stepped inside old Booth draped the saddle and bridle over
a corral pole and called out helpfully, "You'd best throw a
bigger loop, son. I know they look lazy, but once you
commence throwing they can show you some fancy foot-
work indeed."

Stringer moved across the sunny corral toward the
ponies bunched in the meager shade, boasting, "I've been
roping my own mounts since I was big enough to mount
one." But as they began to shuffle their hooves in the dust
and wall-eye him with flared nostrils, Stringer was sorry
he'd shaken out such a modest loop. He could see business
had been slow here, and that the ponies wanted to keep it
that way. But, fool that he was, he'd made a brag without
thinking, and now he had to back it up as best he could.

So he did. The old man over by the gate whistled in
open admiration as Stringer whirled just twice, staring hard
at a paint gelding, then threw at the chestnut just as she

was fixing to snicker at the unfortunate paint.

Blue Ribbon didn't like it much. Stringer had roped her clean but she still fought like a trout, a big one, as he tried to reel her in. His own high heels helped a lot. He still got to step in lots of horseshit and he was dusty to the knees by the time he had the balky pony out the gate and could steady her with a palm cupped to her muzzle. The old man saddled and cinched her, saying, "I admire a man who knows which end of a pony the shit falls outten. What outfits have you rid for?"

Stringer took the bridle and slipped Blue Ribbon's barrel head into it as he replied, "My folk had a spread up in the California Mother Lode range. I haven't been a cowhand for the past few years, though."

Booth said, "I fail to see why. A roper like you could make a dollar a day, most places." Then he added, "Not around here, though. Such outfits as there are here in Cochise County barely make a go of it since the Mexicans wised up."

Stringer asked what he meant by that. The old-timer went on to explain, "Many an outfit in these parts used to, uh, fatten their own herds from stock they found wandering sort of lightly guarded, down Mexico way. We're only a few days drive from the border, you know. But them cussed Mex *rurales* they got patrolling the border these days just refuse to believe in Apache raiders since that damned Tom Horn rounded up all the Apache that time."

Stringer agreed it was getting even harder to make an honest living these days. He led the pony back to where he'd left his gladstone by the old man's house and lashed the bag to the saddle; then he shook hands with the old fellow before mounting up. As he rode off, Booth called after him, "You really ought to have a saddle gun if you mean to stray far off the beaten path, son. The Apache may be tamer, now, but there's still some Mex and even Anglo boys around here that you just don't want to run into, with no more than that *pistol* to back your play."

CHAPTER
FOUR

The wagon trace to Tombstone more or less followed the
now-abandoned and weedy railroad spur that had once
hauled silver ore to the main line. They both passed the
northern end of the Mule Mountains to aim for the higher
peaks of the Dragoons, a fault-block range running north
and south in line with the even higher and more distant
Chiricahuas of Apacheria. Stringer never would have been
on this trail at this time of the day if the distance had been
at all serious. The overhead sun was glaring down from a
cloudless cobalt bowl and it was already hotter than hell's
hinges. He knew that it would be even hotter by, say, three,
because the sun tended to lead its heat by that much.
They'd assured him that, Lord willing and the creeks didn't
rise, he'd be able to reach the shade if not cool of a Tombstone saloon before then, did he lope his pony some.

But while he felt mean enough to trot Blue Ribbon

downhill, when the wagon trace gave them such opportunities, he just didn't have the heart to push her harder in this heat. So it was more like four-thirty and he was sure the poor salt-crusted mare was about to drop under him when they finally staggered in, both walking, and he led her to the first water trough he saw, near the gate of an empty corral on deserted Allen Street, the main thoroughfare of Tombstone. As he watered his mount and resisted the impulse to dive headfirst into the watering trough himself, he told her, soothingly, "I promise we'll ride the other way by moonlight, old girl. If this damned old oven has ever seen a flood it must have been back in Noah's time."

Staring down Allen Street through the shimmering heat waves, he saw the town of Tombstone was indeed still intact. Most of the buildings in sight were thick-walled 'dobes, albeit endowed with frame wooden awnings and plank walks to provide the creature comforts of an Anglo community. Few Mexicans who lived in towns of 'dobe were dumb enough to *need* sidewalks when it was raining or the sun was overhead.

He saw wooden signs jutting out at Allen Street, but he had trouble reading any of them in the shimmering glare. He told his thirsty pony, "That's about enough. I'll just lead you on up till we come to a saloon so I can wet my own poor whistle."

He hauled her head up, with some effort, and began to lead her deeper into town, afoot. He was mildly surprised, when they came to the first patch of awning shade, to see an old geezer sitting on a nail keg, whittling. As if he'd read Stringer's mind, the old-timer said, "It's just as hot indoors. You want to buy a memento of the famous battle, carved from genuine wood from the O.K. Corral?"

Stringer paused with a polite glance down at the pima basket near the old man's right foot. It was half-filled with little wooden six-guns. He said, "You whittle pretty good. But if that was the famous O.K. Corral I just watered at, it seemed to have all its poles, no offense."

The old man replied, "That was the Dexter Corral. I watched you come in, wondering why you was acting so loco. I got me the wood when they repaired the O.K. with new poles. It's that one, catty-corner from the Dexter."

Stringer followed the imaginary line the old man drew with his knife blade and, sure enough, there did seem to be another corral catty-corner from the one he'd watered at. The old man spat. "I get a dime apiece for these here wooden guns. They'll charge you more than that at the O.K. Corral, just for a plain old splinter, the lying bastards," he fumed.

Stringer reached in his jeans for some change as he said, "To tell the truth, I've sort of outgrown toy guns, sir. But I'll buy one if you'll throw in directions to the nearest places I can buy a beer and send a telegram, in that order."

The old man took Stringer's dime with a triumphant smile and said, "Gotcha. The Alhambra Saloon's a grocery, now. But just you keep going and you'll come to the Oriental, which is still serving booze and, hell, Coca-Cola if you want one. As for sending a telegram, I'd try the Western Union, near where the trains used to stop when the trains was still running."

Stringer thanked him, but before heading off asked, "What was that 'gotcha' all about? Are you saying I've been swindled on this fine example of wood carving?"

Grinning up at him, the old man explained, "I never lie, outright. That'd be no fun. These guns I whittle are pure cedar from a pole that once graced the O.K. Corral. It was them, not me, who started greening the tourists with fairy tales about the Earps and Clantons."

Stringer said, "I've heard of their famous shoot-out at the O.K. Corral. Are you saying it never happened?"

The old man looked disgusted. "Sure it happened," he said. "Only it never happened in no O.K. Corral. I was there. Just watching, of course. They had it out in a vacant lot across Fremont Street from the dang corral. But now they got a fool sign posted over at the O.K. Corral, bragging that the fight took place there and offering a look around for a nickel."

Stringer thanked his would-be mentor gravely and led Blue Ribbon on up the dusty street. When he came to an open doorway from which the sounds of tinkling glasses and a busted piano could be heard, he tethered his mount out front and strode in. It turned out he was in the tap room of the Cosmopolitan Hotel instead of the Oriental Saloon, but he said he just didn't care and ordered a boilermaker.

As the elderly barkeep served Stringer he noticed the bitty wooden gun the stranger had placed carelessly on the bar. He nodded. "I see Gramp Ewing got to you first," he said. "I didn't think you'd been here before, no offense."

Smiling sheepishly, Stringer said, "None taken. It's no secret that I'm new in town. You can call me Stringer MacKail; I write for the *San Francisco Sun*. They sent me to cover the big flood you were supposed to have had here. I'm beginning to suspect that old whittler down the way isn't the only one who's been offering odd opinions on recent Tombstone history."

The barkeep made a sour face. "Gramp Ewing is hard to top when it comes to bullshit. Did he just tell you he was present when the Earps and Clantons shot it out that time?"

Stringer nodded. The barkeep shook his head wearily and said, "He ain't been in town five years, the lying old drifter. Anyone you meet here who tells you he was just standing there, watching, is another damned liar and you can tell him I said so."

Another old-timer staring into his glass down the bar cackled, chiming in, "Ain't that the truth? Nobody with a lick of sense would have been just standing within a city block of that loco bastard, Holliday, when he was likkered up and packing a sawed-off shotgun. Virgil Earp was sort of dangerous to be around, as well, now that I study on it."

Stringer sipped some more suds. Then he said, "I'm sure this place was wild as they say, in boom times. But to tell the truth I wasn't sent all this way to cover gunfights old enough to vote. Who might you boys suspect of sending us a whopper about Tombstone getting wiped out by a ferocious flood a few days ago?"

The barkeep shrugged. "I've heard some whoppers told about this town, but that's a new one on me. It ain't even rained here since, let's see, last winter?"

The lone drinker down the bar tried, "What if they meant the Lucky Cuss? It do seem to flood every time they think they got it half-drained, you know."

The piano stopped abruptly. The young, lean, and mean-looking gent who'd been trying to pick out some tune on it spun around on the piano stool to snap, "You talk too fucking much, Woody!"

Woody, if that was the solitary drinker's name, turned a paler shade of gray as he protested, mildly, "Hell, everyone knows the durned old mines are flooded, Knuckles."

The would-be piano player rose to a full six feet and

then some, talking to old Woody but staring at Stringer as he growled, "What happens in Tombstone is Tombstone's own business, and this dude just up and *said* he worked for a damned *newspaper!*"

Stringer stared back just as friendly as he digested that part about him being a dude. The bully by the piano wasn't dressed any more cow than he was. If anything, the rascal was dressed a mite fancier, with silver conchos all over his slate-gray charro outfit in place of sensible buttons. The Colt .45 he packed low on his left hip was silver mounted, too. Its position betrayed him as a southpaw. The grips would have been facing forward if he'd been a cross-draw fighter. Stringer was tempted to see if he was a fighter at all. But despite all the recent war talk he'd heard, this *was* the twentieth century and the law had sort of frowned on such kid stuff back when it had been much easier to get away with. So he decided it was best to say, "Let's not get our bowels in an uproar, gents. I just said I wasn't here to rake up ancient history."

Then he turned back to the barkeep to ask, "Do they have a stable out back, seeing this is a hotel?"

The barkeep looked dubious as he answered, "Yes and no. Guests at the Cosmopolitan are allowed to keep their horses out back. Folk just in town for the day generally use the Dexter or O.K. corrals just down the way."

Before Stringer could reply that he wasn't planning on hiring any hotel rooms, Knuckles stepped ominously closer, saying, "You won't be staying here or at any other hotel in town if you know what's good for you, stranger."

Stringer smiled thinly, picked up the little wooden pistol, and held it out to Knuckles, saying, "Oh, boy, do we get to play cowboys and Indians? Here, you be the cowboy and I'll be the Indian."

Knuckles scowled, reached for the bit of cedar with his right hand, and, as Stringer had supposed he might, reached for his .45 with his left. But since Stringer had been expecting that, just as he'd been smart enough to hold out the taunting toy with his own left, Knuckles found himself staring down the muzzle of Stringer's S&W with his own gun only halfway clear of its low-slung holster. Nobody present breathed as Knuckles simply slid his side arm back into its holster and smiled weakly, asking, "Jesus, can't you take a joke?"

Stringer's smile was a lot less insecure as he replied, "Not unless they strike me funny. One humorous son of a bitch has drug me all the way down here on a snipe hunt for no reason I can grasp. Now another son of a bitch just offered to run me out of a town I never wanted to come to in the first place. So I ask you, one and all, should I be laughing right now?"

Glowering, Knuckles told him flatly, "I ain't sure I like to be called a son of a bitch, MacKail."

Stringer put his own pistol back in its holster before he growled, "I'm sorry to hear that, you son of a bitch. We're back on the starting line again, fair and square. So let's see you fish or cut bait, you son, I repeat, of a mighty mangy bitch."

Knuckles gulped, turned on one heel, and marched out with his hands out polite, not looking back.

The barkeep let his breath out explosively and said, "I never expected Knuckles Ashton to crawfish like that. But, then, I never expected lots of wonders I've seen out this way. You'd best consider quitting while you're ahead,

MacKail. I know where that old boy's headed. You got mayhaps a quarter-hour to vamoose, hear?"

Old Woody, down the bar, opined morosely, "Quarter-hour could be cutting it too fine. I'd be leaving *now* if I just called Knuckles Ashton a son of a bitch and was still alive!"

Stringer said, "I think I'll have another drink. Just beer, this time. Where do you boys think he's headed, to call the law on me?"

The barkeep poured more draft, but said with a sigh, "You really are new in town. Didn't you hear they moved the county seat down to Bisbee when the mines here in Tombstone bottomed out?"

Stringer shook his head. "That doesn't surprise me. The Bisbee mines are sort of famous. That would be about twenty miles south of here, right?"

Old Woody said, "More like twenty-five, as the crow flies. A harder ride aboard anything else. Knuckles Ashton never went to Bisbee to report you to no sheriff, son. He's headed for the Oriental Saloon, where a jasper called Skagway Sam is riding herd on all the gambling concessions. Knuckles and his gun work for Skagway Sam. I wouldn't call Skagway Sam *'sweetheart'* with the sheriff such a long ways off, if I was you."

When nothing had happened for close to an hour, Stringer went next door to the hotel lobby and hired room and board for both him and his pony. When the clerk asked how long he'd be in town Stringer said he didn't know. He paid a day in advance and still had to tip a Mex kid to take his gladstone up to his room and then tip another two out back to make sure they put Blue Ribbon in her stall rubbed down as well as watered and fed. Then he cut back around to the front and headed up Allen Street for the Western Union office.

The broad dusty street was devoid of traffic. The place sure looked like a totally ghosted town, even though he now knew at least a few old-timers were somehow holding on. He assumed the surrounding cow spreads offered at least some trade to the once bustling community. Still, he noticed that more than half the storefronts he passed were boarded up. Cowhands didn't spend nearly as much as mining men and few of them got to town as often as once a week.

He'd just paused to study his own reflection in a shop window, noting how badly he needed a shave, when he caught movement out of the corner of one eye. He turned to go on, even though a line of seven men on foot stood silently in the shimmering heat, from one side of Allen to the other. He recognized the two holding down the center of the street with their bootheels as if they thought they owned it. He knew any number of witnesses were watching from the curtained windows all around and he knew how confused accounts of a fight could be when they didn't take place out in plain sight. So he stepped off the walk to approach Skagway Sam and Knuckles Ashton at an angle, his gun hand hovering out to one side as he closed the distance between himself and whatever the hell all these idiots aimed to do in broad-ass daylight.

As the bully he'd confronted and then saved recognized the approaching Stringer, he huffed, "Oh, it's you. I might have known."

Stringer stopped at easy, albeit not point-blank, pistol range to call back, "Howdy, Skagway. It's nice to see *you* again so soon, Knuckles. What did you do, tell the teacher on me?"

"Now you're gonna get it," Knuckles growled.

But Skagway Sam shushed him with a lazy wave of one big paw and called out to Stringer, "You got me sort of confused, old son. I can't say I admire your manners, but you did save my ass in the Tucson yards the other night. Are we supposed to consider our fool selves friends or enemies?"

"Dealer's choice," Stringer replied with a lift of his shoulders, "seeing you seem to be the big deal around here. I got no quarrel with any man who's willing to just leave me the hell alone. Just now, I was on my way to send some telegrams. You got any objection to that, Skagway Sam?"

The burly gambling boss replied, soberly, "*I* got no problem with that, MacKail. My problem is that you just now throwed down on one of my boys. Knuckles, here, says you got the drop on him some sneaky way and made him look dumb."

Stringer shot back, "He is dumb. He's a liar, too, if he says I backed him down unfair. Want to see me do it again?"

There was an ominous growl from the other gunslicks assembled to either side, but Skagway Sam waved his paw some more and told Stringer, in a sincerely interested tone, "I surely would. Are you proposing a *mano a mano*, just you and Knuckles, with nothing up nobody's sleeve?"

Stringer replied, "I don't know what he might or might not have up his sleeve. I got this one S and W, hanging in plain sight. Now, with your permission, I'd like to call

Knuckles a son of a bitch again, and see what he aims to do about it."

Skagway Sam agreed, "That sounds fair." Then he moved clear of Knuckles as the gunslick on Ashton's far side did the same.

Stringer asked, soberly, "How about it, Knuckles?"

The silver-trimmed Knuckles turned to his boss with a pleading look to blurt out, "He's got some trick kind of holster or something. You ain't seen him draw, boss!"

Skagway Sam said, "I know. That's what we're all fixing to see. What are you waiting on, Knuckles? Didn't you just hear the man refer to you as a son of a bitch?"

Knuckles shook his head like a stubborn child refusing castor oil as he blubbered, "Dammit, I come to you boys for *help*, not to put on a suicide exhibition for nobody!"

Skagway Sam nodded. Then he said, "You're fired, Knuckles. Don't let the sun set on you in this town." He turned back to Stringer and said, "You go on and send all the telegrams you want. Just don't call *me* no son of a bitch. I'm sore tempted to find out if you could be half as ferocious as you and this crybaby seem to think you are. But, like I said, I owe you for the other night. So don't mess with me and mine and we won't mess with you, deal?"

"Deal." Then Stringer walked on through their politely parted line. The space between his sweaty shoulder blades itched like hell until he was out of pistol range, but he didn't look back. He just marched up the center of Allen Street as if he owned it, until he got to the Western Union sign and marched that way, for what felt like a hundred miles. When at last he was inside, he gripped the counter with both hands and gasped, "Whoosh! I sure am surprised to be in here."

The clerk behind the counter replied, "I'm surprised, too. We don't do much business, this time of the day. You look sort of sick to your stomach, mister. You could be suffering a touch of sun stroke, if you want my opinion."

Stringer got his breathing back under control and told the concerned clerk, "As a matter of fact I'm just getting over a bad case of goose bumps. But since I'm still alive, I'd like to send a wire to San Francisco."

The clerk slid him a pad of yellow telegram blanks and a pencil. As he block-lettered his terse message to Sam Barca, Stringer asked if a young lady answering to Matilda Gower had sent or received any messages of late. The clerk sounded sincere when he allowed he'd never heard the name before. Stringer asked if they had a library in Tombstone and the clerk said, "Sure. Courthouse square, if it's still in business. They shut down the courthouse when they moved the county seat down to Bisbee. Such local hearings as they still hold here are sort of scootched into City Hall with the town marshal. How come you need a library if you ain't from around here? I doubt they'll let you take any books out without a local library card."

Stringer slid his message across the counter to the clerk as he said, "I'm more worried about a librarian I know than a library. How soon can I expect an answer to this wire?"

The clerk shot a glance at the big clock on the wall before he replied, "Say two or three if your party wires back direct." Then, since he had to count the words to set a fee, he did so and objected, in a hurt tone, "A man's entitled to his own opinion. But we like to think Tombstone's too tough to die. Don't you think you're putting it a mite strong when you call Tombstone bone-dry and dead as ever?"

Stringer assured him no insult to his fair metropolis was intended, explaining, "We were told you'd had a big flood here, with lots of damage to lives and property. As anyone can plainly see, there's a heap of real estate out there for sale, cheap, and, no offense, there aren't many people to drown if and when you ever do have a flood."

"The population swells a good deal of a Saturday night. Even when the cowhands ain't in town we must have close to a thousand permanent residents," the clerk sniffed.

Stringer asked, "How many did Tombstone shelter before the mines bottomed out?"

The somewhat older clerk sighed wistfully and replied, "Oh, Lord, fifteen thousand or more, even weeknights. Tombstone was the biggest city in Arizona Territory in its day. Lord knows where all them have gone, the fickle sons of bitches. It were just after the war with Spain when the Lucky Cuss shut down. Then the Tough Nut bottomed out and lots of the boys working the smaller shafts didn't even wait to get their last notices. One morning there was fifteen thousand men, women, and children of all ages. Then, all of a sudden, there wasn't."

Stringer said, "That would have been just about the time the first reports of color up Alaska way were coming in. I reckon I'd have quit a failing silver mine and joined a gold rush if I didn't know better. I see at least two shady characters of the Alaska rush have wandered back. I'll be back around three, anyway. I just can't wait until this town comes back to life again."

He went back outside. It was even hotter now. He knew that if he went back to his hotel for a siesta he'd have a hell of a time falling asleep and if he did he'd wake up cranky and out of sorts. He needed a shave, and a haircut wouldn't kill him. Doing anything had wandering around in the Arizona sun beat by miles.

The sun had crawled across the cloudless sky enough to offer at least a shady patch yonder and about. Stringer found a corner barber shop that wasn't being baked too badly and went in to find that other great minds had run in the same channels. There were a couple of gents ahead of him.

Like the bald barber and just about everyone else he'd seen so far in Tombstone, they were much older than he was. He saw that they, as well as the old gent in the one barber's chair, had hung their gun rigs along with their hats on hooks along the plastered 'dobe wall. He hung up his Roughrider hat but wasn't ready to get that far from his side arm just yet. As he sat down on a bentwood chair, adjusting his holster so it hung less awkwardly over the edge of his hard seat, he kept his peace and rolled a smoke. The old-timers took only a few minutes to get used to his presence and, just as birds are inclined to resume chirping once they see a housecat on a back porch is just sitting there, they commenced to go on living in the past or on hopes for the future.

Stringer didn't join in. He'd been around enough to know that regulars tended to include a newcomer when they damn well felt like it and resented a pushy stranger. He doubted any of them could tell him anything he really wanted to know about Tombstone to begin with. But as he sat there, silently smoking, he learned more than he really wanted to know, anyway. He didn't grasp some of the laconic gossip about people he didn't know; but he could follow the drift well enough to learn, or confirm, that Tombstone was barely hanging on because of economic factors none of the old gents might have understood, had he been dumb enough to lecture them.

Thanks to that one Stanford course they'd made him take whether he wanted to or not, Stringer knew that while towns had to be created by mankind, once they'd grown to a certain size, they sort of took on a life of their own, like a fungus or a cancer.

Tombstone had been spawned by death, when two unknown prospectors had been jumped by Apache in the foothills of the Dragoons. After the Apache and the buzzards had finished with them, their bones had just sun-bleached there for an unknown number of years. Eventually Indian scout Ed Schieffelin, prospecting on his own in an area he'd been warned would be the death of him, spotted something white in the chaparral, had a closer look, and found not only the skeletons lying head to head, but a pile of silver ore the Apache had no doubt dismissed as worthless rocks the white eyes had meant to make medicine with.

It didn't take an old scout like Schieffelin long to backtrack the original discoveries to their nearby and already opened silver vein. With the backing of a more prosperous brother, the sardonic Schieffelin recorded his strike as the Tombstone mine. By the spring of '79 the Schieffelin brothers had struck the even richer Lucky Cuss and Tough Nut veins, and then, having planted the spore of a town where only Apache had roamed before, the now-wealthy brothers sold out and played no further part in the mushroom growth of the mining camp down the slopes.

They didn't have to. Given any reason for being there, a

town just grows. Drawn by dreams of easy money, folk flocked in from all directions; via Texas Canyon, Dragoon Gap, and Mustang Pass they came. They poured over the Mogollon Rim, covered wagons and all, or along the Apache-haunted Camino del Diablo. Many who chose that route never made it. By the end of the year the town was a worthy rival of Tucson and demanding its right to serve as the county seat. The territorial governor, appointed by the Republican Hayes administration, solved that problem in a manner worthy of Solomon. He simply cut the original Pima County in two and let both towns serve as county seat. Both Pima and the newer Cochise County would reward the Republicans by ever after voting almost solid Democrat.

Thus it came to pass that by the turn of the century, with little or no help from the ruffians who'd be remembered longer than its mines, Tombstone was still there. It lived on, however modestly. Stringer knew it could never again be the boom town the old-timers were mooning about, but should they manage not to blow it up or burn it down, Tombstone was there to stay, if only as a market town and entertainment center for the surrounding cattle outfits. He thought their notion of making the Bird Cage Opera House the biggest and wildest whorehouse in the territory sounded like a pipe dream. He was too polite to say so, and after a time it was his turn in the chair.

By the time the old barber was draping the seersucker sheet over Stringer some other customers had come in to occupy the vacant seats and wall hooks. One younger rider, dressed more cow, hung up an S&W .38 that could have come from the same litter as Stringer's. He said he'd just ridden in and that the range was so dry he'd been afraid to smoke on the trail. Stringer knew one of the others would ask him how the stock was doing and that he'd say poorly. Nobody ever admitted to owning fat cows this close to the border.

The old barber asked Stringer the usual polite questions as he lathered and shaved him, but then he plopped a hot towel over Stringer's face without waiting for an answer. Stringer usually shaved himself and, in any case, it was just too damned hot to enjoy the scalding. So he sat up straight and removed the hot towel himself, muttering, "That felt swell. Now, if you'd just trim the sides..." Then he noticed Knuckles Ashton had come in for his own barbering while he'd been under the towel. Knuckles looked equally surprised as they locked eyes. Nodding pleasantly, Stringer said, "Howdy. I sure hope we've got things settled between us, Knuckles."

Knuckles got to his feet, ready to say he'd come back later, most likely. Then he spotted the otherwise innocent S&W hanging on the wall a lot closer to him than to Stringer, and slid between the barber chair and gun, grinning like a coyote who'd just spied a newborn lamb with nary a sheepherder in sight. His sinister move wasn't lost on the old barber, who'd no doubt been barbering in Tombstone some time. He stopped Stringer's haircut before he'd started it with a snip of his scissors and the warning, "Hold on, Ashton. If you boys have something to settle, I sure wish you'd take it outside."

Knuckles growled, "Shut up and stand clear unless you want the same, old man. That goes for everyone else in here. I got a lot to settle with this old boy. Ain't that true, MacKail?"

Stringer said, soberly, "Far be it from me to call a man

who seems to have the drop on me a liar. But we'd better study on this situation, Knuckles. I hope you and all these other gents can see I came in here for a shave and a haircut, *ahead* of you."

Knuckles just went on looking mean and dumb, so Stringer elaborated, "This is a barber shop, not the O.K. Corral, and even then the winners got run out of town in the end."

Knuckles grinned slyly. "That's all right. I was fixing to leave town by sundown in any case. But first I aim to settle the score with you."

By this time the barber had moved over to a far corner and the two remaining customers were cowering in another. The braggart who had the floor shot a last quick look at that hung-up S&W before he muttered, "If you got any last words, you'd best say 'em now, MacKail."

Stringer said, "Knuckles, you're sure making an awesome mistake. Why don't we drop this kid stuff before someone gets hurt?"

Knuckles took a deep breath, said, "I'll just show you who's a kid around here!" and went for his .45, left-handed.

Naturally, Stringer had been holding his .38 in his right hand for some time. So as he fired, thrice, double-action, the burly southpaw spun on one bootheel and dove head-first through the plate-glass front of the barber shop to wind up on the walk outside, covered and cut up by shattered glass and squealing like a stuck pig.

Stringer whipped off the seersucker sheet and rolled out of the chair, smoking six-gun in hand, to leap through the now-glass-free storefront and land almost atop his victim. He failed to see how a dead man could be making so much noise, so he hunkered down to disarm Knuckles before he soothed, "Aw, shut up, you can't be hurt that bad."

Knuckles pounded on the walk with one bloody fist, sobbing, "Now you've done it! You've kilt me and my poor old mother will never get to see her baby again."

The barber stuck his head out, warily, to ask how bad it might be. Stringer said, "I'm sorry about your powder-burned seersucker and busted window. I'll be proud to pay for both, even if the window wasn't entirely my fault."

The barber said, "I was talking about Knuckles, there."

Stringer began to reload as he replied, "Oh, he's just hit in his shoulder, hip, and ass. It's hard as hell to aim off-hand with drapery all over your muzzle."

By this time, despite the ovenlike afternoon heat, others were moving in from all sides. When Stringer spotted Skagway Sam in the crowd he lowered his .38 to his side but didn't holster it. But it was an older and skinnier gent with a brass star pinned to the lapel of his undertaker-looking outfit who first demanded an explanation of the recent noise and the moaning results at Stringer's feet.

The old barber called back, "For God's sake don't draw on *this* gent, Wes! Even if you could take him, he was in the right. I was just now trying to give him a haircut when Ashton, there, told one and all he intended to kill him, premeditated, with results you can see with your own eyes."

The town law joined Stringer above the bleeding and braying Knuckles to observe, mildly, "I've been expecting this one to wind up dead, or hung as the winner. I don't believe I know you at all, old son."

Stringer holstered his six-gun and hauled out his credentials. As the lawman called Wes scanned them, Skagway Sam came over to stare soberly down at the mess at their feet. He said, "Some boys just never learn. I'd just fired Knuckles as a gutless troublemaker, Marshal. But for old time's sake, I'll get a doc on my payroll to patch him up."

Wes said, dryly, "He could use some patching. Are we talking about that old abortionist who looks after the whores you and Faro Fran have working at the Oriental, now?"

Skagway Sam smiled good-naturedly. "Somebody has to. By the way, I'm a gambler, not a pimp. My, ah, companion, Faro Fran, runs that concession. I doubt old Knuckles here needs to be treated for the clap or an unwanted offspring. But the doc treated gunshot wounds in the War Between the States and, hell, it won't cost the town nothing, whether he dies or not."

Wes said that sounded fair, but shot a thoughtful look at Stringer as he handed back the billfold, saying, "Skagway may not care if this gent you just shot makes it or not. But we do have some rules, here in Tombstone. I hope you wasn't planning on leaving town in the near future, Mr. MacKail."

Stringer cursed under his breath before he replied, "As a matter of fact I was planning on riding back to the rail line this evening, with permission of my boss, as soon as I got it. I take it you and the county coroner are willing to suspend judgment, one way or the other, until this silly bastard figures out whether to live or die on us?"

"That's about the size of it," Wes agreed. "The coroner as well as the county sheriff are down in Bisbee right now. They let us run things, up this way, unless they get really serious. I can't see Knuckles pressing assault charges against you and I take it you don't want me to arrest him for assaulting you, just now?"

Stringer shook his head vigorously. "Hell, no," he yelped. "I can't wait to be on my way as it is. How long do you figure I'll be stuck here, Marshal?"

The older man said, "It's up to old Knuckles, here. If he dies, you could be stuck here quite a spell."

CHAPTER
FIVE

Things got worse when Stringer stopped by the Western Union office just after three to find a reply from his feature editor waiting for him. The cranky old bastard said he was backtracking that wire-service false alarm about the great flood and that, meanwhile, Stringer should stay put, in case there was someone the *Sun* wanted beat up. Barca suggested that as long as he was on the scene, a rehash of the famous feud between the Earp and Clanton factions might be worth running in the Sunday supplement if Stringer could come up with a fresh angle or, better yet, some hitherto unpublished photographs.

Stringer balled the wire up with a growl of dismissal. But as he cooled off with a cold Coca-Cola on the shady porch of the grocery across the way, he couldn't help adding up the space rates of a two- or three-page Sunday feature. At least something or other had once happened somewhere around the O.K. Corral. That was more than the man-eating giant artichoke of Madagascar could say, and Jack London was cleaning up with his man-eating wolves along the Yukon. So in hopes of hitting two birds with one more walk in the hot sun, Stringer headed for the library near the old county courthouse.

The library was still open after all and, better yet, the gal on duty was some pumpkin, if you didn't mind horn-rim specs. He figured her for about twenty-five, built right to pose for old Charles Dana Gibson, but not with all that auburn hair. She had it pinned atop her head in the current style, but Stringer suspected it fell way past her behind when she let it down. He warned himself not to picture a gal who was already good-looking enough standing bare-ass with her hair down. He ticked his hat brim to her and began by asking if another librarian answering to Tillie Gower had ever shown up.

She stared back through her specs, puzzled, and allowed she'd never heard the name, that she was the only librarian they still had, and that while her name was Iona Fraser she preferred to be called Annie. He nodded, knowingly, and said, "I was saddled with a West Highland handle, too. *Comair e tha thu?*"

She replied, *"Tha mi gu math,* and if it's all the same to you I'm trying to live it down, Mr. ah . . . ?"

"Stuart MacKail, but call me Stringer," he replied.

Annie dimpled and said, "I don't blame you. If your people were like mine you were raised on the same tales of blood and slaughter."

"To tell the truth," he said, laughing, "I came here this afternoon to look up more recent feuding and fussing. I write for the *San Francisco Sun* and they want a rehash of the Earp and Clanton feud here in Tombstone."

She made a wry face—her nose was pretty, even wrinkled up—and said, "Oh, Lord, let's talk about the MacDonalds and the Macleods, in the Old Country. At least they had *reasons* to kill one another. I've been hearing about those silly Earps and Clantons since I was a child and they still don't make any sense."

He counted backwards, mentally, and said, "Far be it from me to ask a lady's age, Miss Annie, but is it safe to assume you could have been here, sort of young, on that fatal day in the October of 1881?"

She bobbed her head as she replied, "I was in the first grade, as a matter of fact. My late father was a foreman at the Lucky Cuss and my Uncle Murdoch was timekeeper at the Tough Nut."

He said, "Anyone can see you come from quality, Miss Annie. But what did you and your little classmates think when you heard about that fight that's become so famous?"

"Nothing," she stated simply. "We never heard about it until we were older. Our parents didn't talk about it at the time. You see, those drunken drifters over on Allen Street were always killing one another. It wasn't a subject of interest to the more civilized residents of Tombstone."

"That sounds reasonable," Stringer agreed. "Back in Frisco the folk on Nob Hill take little interest in the tong wars of our Chinatown. But, dumb as it sounds, my feature editor wants me to pretend it was more serious. So what would you have here on the topic of Tombstone toughs in the good old days?"

She gasped, "Good heavens, this is a library, not a penny-dreadful shop. I think we do have some works by Colonel William Cody and we have an autographed copy of *Ben-Hur,* written by the former governor of New Mexico, Lew Wallace. But books about the likes of Johnny Ringo, Buckskin Frank, that awful Dr. Holliday, and those disgusting Earp brothers? Why on earth would anybody write a book about such no-account residents of this otherwise upright town?"

"Wyatt Earp's wife has," Stringer said, sighing. "I don't know if she's found a publisher, yet. I suspect it's as biased as the back issues of the *Tombstone Nugget* I've read, slanted the other way entire."

She nodded. "Both the *Nugget* and *Epitaph* have always been ferociously partisan. You might try back issues of either the *Tombstone Expositor* or *Evening Gossip*. They never carried as much about the low-life along Allen Street, but when they did they tried to stick to just the facts."

He said, "That's a grand notion, Miss Annie. Where might either of these more reliable newspapers be published, here in town?"

She started to give directions. Then she flustered and said, "Oh, silly me. Since the mines shut down I fear the only paper still in business is the *Epitaph*. But I'm sure they'd let you look through their . . . old files?"

He said, "We call it the morgue in the newspaper game. I fear I don't need the *Epitaph* to assure me the Earps could do wonders, and do no wrong. I've known for some time that old John Clum, the owner of the *Epitaph*, was a drinking pal of Wyatt Earp."

She shook her head and said, "You mean Virgil and Morgan Earp, the older brothers. Young Wyatt was just a sort of tag-along in his Tombstone days. They had some other brothers, I believe. But Virgil and Morgan were the real toughs of the clan."

Stringer muttered, "That's not the way old Wyatt tells it, out L.A. way. But, while we're on the subject, Miss Annie, what do you recall about the Clantons?"

"Nothing. Drunken cowboys were not allowed in our part of town. I can't say I ever met any of those uncouth ruffians. I suppose more people gossiped about the Earps because they lived in town. The Clantons seldom got in to Tombstone enough to draw that much attention to themselves. I just can't say which bunch was worse."

He said that made two of them. He knew he faced a night or more alone at the Cosmopolitan. But without a library card it was likely a waste of time to browse the stacks behind her, so he thanked her for such information as she'd been able to give him and turned to go.

The recent shave paid off when she called him back and said, "I just thought of something. We lend a lot of books to a sweet old man who stayed on when the *Tombstone Expositor* went out of business. I think he was either one of their reporters or printers."

Looking hopeful, Stringer explained, "On small-town papers, reporters are supposed to know how to set type and vice versa. If he was working here in the eighties for an objective publisher he'd be a gold mine."

"That's what I thought," she said, dimpling.

There was an awkward silence. Then Stringer sighed, "Well?"

"I'm thinking," she said, "I'm thinking. If I could re-member his name I could get his address for you from the card file. I know the other old-timers call him Dutchy and I think his last name is Dutch or German. *Och mo mala!* It's right on the tip of my tongue, but—"

"Let it go for now and it will come back to you when you least expect it," Stringer suggested.

"I know," she agreed, "but what good will that do if it comes to me in bed, later tonight?"

He had to laugh and, even though he didn't say why, she blushed and stammered, "That's not the way I meant it, you fresh old thing."

He nodded, shot a glance at the Regulator Brand school clock behind her, and asked what time they closed. She told him they only stayed open after six on Fridays. He said, "Then I'll try to be back before six. If not, well, I'm booked in at the Cosmopolitan on Allen Street."

She gasped, "Heavens! No respectable lady would be caught dead on Allen Street after dark, or by daylight, without an escort. I'd best just give you my own address in case you, ah, miss me."

He didn't argue. He was no fool. She drew a blank card from a whole box of the same and penciled in her name and address in prim Palmer penmanship. As she handed it across the counter to him she said, as primly, "I generally receive visitors no later than eight, or, well, maybe nine."

He carefully tucked the card in a breast pocket and told her he hardly ever kept a lady up past her bedtime. She lowered her lashes and decided, in a firmer tone, "If you don't come by eight I won't be expecting you to come at all."

He didn't think she could mean that the way it sounded, so he just left, wondering what on earth was getting into him all of a sudden. He could usually talk to a lady, an ugly one at any rate, without such horny thoughts. Even when they were pretty it was just asking too much of the great god Eros for him to make it with *two* mild-mannered librarians in a row!

He wondered some more about old Tillie as he wandered back to the center of town. Her story had made a lot more sense when he'd met her in Tucson than it did right now. She'd either lied or been confused as hell about having a library job lined up here in Tombstone. But, either way, what could her real game have been?

Stringer had a healthy ego. He knew lots of women just plain fell for him, just as he knew he couldn't have 'em all. So it was possible, but just barely, that old Tillie had simply wanted to have an affair with him. She for sure hadn't been out to roll him. So she'd been fibbing about being stranded in Tucson with neither her baggage nor pin money. Had she been on that train at all? And, if she had, how could she have seen the shoot-out? He'd been trailing the other passengers when that Mex had thrown down on Skagway Sam and Faro Fran. They, in turn, had been between him, the hired gun, and all the other passengers.

As he entered the lobby of his hotel he muttered, "Someone put her up to it. She never left Tucson. Ergo she was likely local. But how come?"

As he stopped at the desk to pick up his key the clerk on duty told him, "There was a gent asking for you, just now, Mr. MacKail. I told him you were out and asked him if he wanted to leave a message. He just turned around and left, sort of rude."

Stringer pocketed the key as he replied with a frown, "Do tell?? What'd he look like?"

The clerk answered, cautiously, "Sort of mean. I hope

he ain't a pal of yours, but you did ask and I was riz to tell the truth, within reason."

Stringer dug into his jacket pocket to haul out the menu Homer Davenport had drawn on. It was creased up and sweat-stained, now, but as Stringer unfolded it he saw the ink hadn't run too badly. He asked the clerk if the ugly mutt Davenport had drawn could be the jasper they were talking about. The clerk held the wilted menu up to the light before he decided, "I see a sort of family resemblance around the eyes. The one as was just here had brows as met in the middle like that. But, I dunno."

Stringer took the drawing back, saying, "If he comes back, tell him I'm in, only ring me on the house phone before you send him up."

The clerk said he'd be proud to. Then Stringer mounted the stairs and unlocked his hired room to wash up and at least change his shirt and socks after a day of Arizona Territory.

To do so he had to go down the hall to a fairly decent common bath. Running water, even at one end of the building, was still a novelty in Tombstone. The telephone set he'd noticed by his bed wasn't connected up to anything but room service. The hotel lamps, if he wanted to light any, still ran on coal oil. He didn't know whether that meant the town had no electricity at all or whether Miss Annie had been right about Allen Street being sort of unfashionable. The late-afternoon sunlight through the frosted window of the bath made that point sort of pointless. The tap water came out the same way whether one twisted hot or cold. That didn't much matter, either, since the water tank on the roof produced water that was about the temperature and, come to think of it, the color, of stale tea. He got himself clean as he could, dried off, and dressed again. He was just strapping on his gun rig when the floor under him and the walls around him were rocked by a tremendous crash.

A bolt of dry lightning seemed improbable. That left a man-made detonation and, as he opened the door, he only had to take one whiff of nitro fumes to know some joker had just set off some dynamite. Close. So he drew his S&W and advanced through the blue haze until he got to the open door of his hotel room. He hadn't left it open. Someone had opened it to toss the dynamite bomb inside. The air was too filled with nitro fumes and feathers to make out all the details, but the windowpanes had been blown out and if there was anything to that superstition about mirrors, the bomber had just assured himself seven years of bad luck.

Stringer was just making sure his gladstone, in the closet, hadn't suffered any damage when the room clerk and a couple of other gents with drawn guns came in to join him. The clerk gave an anguished gasp and said, "Holy shit! What was you smoking in bed, just now, Mr. MacKail?"

Stringer replied, "Lucky for me, I was down the hall washing up. I reckon the son of a bitch just lit the fuse, popped the door open, and threw without looking."

The clerk stared morosely at the torn-up bed, saying, "Son of a bitch is too nice a term for the murderous motherfucker! It was that same one. The one I told you about. He came back and, like you said to, I told him you was in and gave him the room number. I rang the phone at you, but . . . Say, where in the hell *is* that telephone?"

Stringer said, "Blown back to the Bell factory for repairs, most likely. I get the picture, now. I'm just damn glad he didn't know I was in the bath. New plumbing could cost like hell."

The four of them had just put their guns away when Wes Rhodes, the town law, came in to join them, staring about in wonder as he put his own gun away and observed, "I might have known you'd be mixed up in all that noise, MacKail. What in thunder's going on up here? There's busted glass halfway across the street outside!"

Stringer told him it had been an infernal device and made an educated guess at who the intended target had been. Old Wes said, "I'd run you out of town if I knew for sure that Knuckles Ashton was gonna make it. It wasn't him, by the way. They got him in bed over to the Oriental, wrapped up like a mummy and full of opium and chicken soup. I just paid a call on him, less than a quarter-hour ago."

Stringer hauled out the menu again as he said, "A gent who looked a lot like this drawing may have sent a wire ahead of me from Soledad, California. The clerk, here, says a gent who could be related to him by eyebrows done the dirty deed with the dynamite. How do you like one brother, or kissing cousin, overhearing me say I was on my way to Tombstone just before he wired the one here that I was coming?"

Wes Rhodes spat out a feather that had drifted into his mouth and said, "I don't like it at all. But it makes sense. I don't suppose it's occurred to you that Skagway Sam and Faro Fran just came back from some business deal they had in California?"

Stringer's amber eyes were big-cat cold as he nodded

grimly. "It has. I reckon I'd better have another little talk
with Skagway Sam," he declared.

It was easier said than done. The Oriental Saloon was only
a short walk from the hotel. But when Stringer parted the
bat wings and strode up to the bar the bald and bullet-
headed barkeep told him the boss gambler had just stepped
out for supper. When Stringer asked where Skagway Sam
generally ate, the burly barkeep merely shrugged. "I
wouldn't know," he claimed. "I just work here. Did you
come in for a drink, a game of chance, or to get laid? We
don't serve *gossip,* here."

Stringer ordered a beer. As the barkeep worked the tap,
Stringer had time to run a casual eye over his surroundings.
No lamps were lit, yet, making the interior of the Oriental
darker this close to sunset than it would be later. There
wasn't much of a crowd. Most of the suppertime drinkers
were old and rather seedy-looking. But, in a far corner, the
brassy Faro Fran was holding court, or at least dealing
faro, at a corner table. Stringer paid for his schooner,
picked it up, and ambled over.

As he drew close enough to make out the features of the
painted adventuress and her two well-dressed but old and
lonely-looking players, he could see she used lots of henna
in her hair as well as makeup on her face. She looked more
like a painted china doll than a woman of flesh and blood.
She didn't look up to meet his eyes as she asked him in a
coarse whiskey tenor whether he'd come over to play cards
or to stare down the front of her low-cut bodice.

He said, "Neither, no offense. I'm looking for Skagway.
I don't suppose you'd know where I could find him at this
hour?"

Shrugging her bare shoulders, she asked, "How should I know? Do I look like his mother?"

Stringer chuckled. "Not hardly. You may not remember me. We sort of met on the train from L.A. to Tucson the other night."

She dealt another card from the slipper on the green felt between them before she said, "I remember you. You smoke too much. You might try the Hatch Billiard Parlor if you just have to blow more Bull Durham in Sam's face. He likes to shoot a game or two of pool to settle an early supper. He don't get much exercise after dark, unless he catches somebody cheating in here."

Stringer thanked her, put his half-finished beer back on the bar, and left. As he started down the street toward the pool hall a rat-faced kid left the side door of the Oriental to dart that way ahead of him. It made finding the right pool hall only that much easier.

Warned or not, Skagway Sam seemed intent on sinking the ten ball, bent low over the pool table in his vest and shirtsleeves, when Stringer entered. Skagway Sam shot, sank what he was aiming at, and, without looking up, asked, "What can I do for you, this evening, MacKail?"

Stringer said, "I got a little puzzle I thought you might like to help me out with, Sam."

The burly gambler replied, "I just heard about the way they messed up your bed. Infernal devices ain't my style. The results can be too unpredictable, as you and your playmates just found out. You want to join me in a game of rotation?"

Stringer nodded, hung his hat and jacket on a hook near the racks, but left his gun on as he selected a cue and moved back to the table. Skagway Sam was already rack-ing the balls to start afresh. Stringer chalked his cue tip, thoughtfully, as he said, "Just before we met in that club car the other night I got glared at by another gent aboard another train."

Skagway Sam said, "You ought to smoke another brand of tobacco then. It was the lady I was with as found Bull Durham so obnoxious, by the way. She don't smoke and she don't chew and she don't screw with boys who do. Nickel a point to make this more interesting?"

"Sure," Stringer agreed. "What I'm really interested in is why folk keep trying to kill me, ever since I was over-heard saying I was bound for Tombstone to write a newspaper feature on the same."

Skagway Sam said, "Why don't you go first? I never sent poor Knuckles after you. Old Fran thinks it might have been jealousy as first set him off. We was sort of singing your praises on arrival, and Jesus Garcia had a rep as well. I figure Knuckles was out to build a rep of his own. Lord knows he sure could use one. He talks a better fight than he fights."

Stringer bent low over the table with his cue, knowing the gambler's apparent generosity was motivated by the simple fact that the pool shooter who opened the rack seldom sank anything with his first shot. Skagway Sam simply wanted him to spread the tightly racked balls apart so that *he* could sink one or more.

Stringer slammed the cue ball as hard as he could into the yellow one ball. By sheer luck the ten ball went in as they all rolled madly in every direction. That gave Stringer a chance to hit the one ball again and sink the three ball. In rotation you got to sink any fool ball as long as you hit the lowest number left on the table first. He missed his third shot and straightened up, chalking his cue tip again as he asked, casually, "How did you know it was Jesus Garcia the two of us shot in the piss-poor light of the Tucson yards, Sam?"

The gambler bent over the table, saying, "Easy. I was told. Ain't you never heard of Western Union, old son? Seven in the side pocket. Shit, I thought I had it."

Stringer bent over to sink the one ball. He was getting tired of looking at it. He aimed next to sink the two ball, just missed doing so, and said, "Who wired you the glad tidings from Tucson, a mousy little gal called Tillie?"

Laughing, the gambler said, rather smugly, "If you just have to know, I got a pal on the Tucson force. You got a vivid imagination, that's what *you* got. Has it slipped your mind that Garcia was aiming at *me*, not *you*, that night?"

Stringer shook his head. "Nope. I just said it was a puzzle. Almost anyone who's ever gambled against you might have a reason for wanting you dead. I've been busting my brains trying to figure out why they seem to be after me as well. I never said anything about Tombstone in front of either that first sneak or the mysterious Tillie that's not common public knowledge. All I've found out since I got here is that the town's half-dead and that can hardly be a secret worth even one attempt on my life."

Skagway Sam ran three balls in a row before he missed, stood taller to chalk his own cue, and said, "Try her this way. *Nobody* was after you before you blew Jesus Garcia off my back, for which I said I thanked you. Garcia was a hired killer. His breed tends to run in packs. Don't it stand to reason that some pal of his was out to pay you back and, respecting your proven skill with a six-gun, decided it might be safer just to blow you up?"

"Nope. Garcia was after you to begin with. We both put a bullet in him. You and Miss Faro Fran beat me here to Tombstone by almost twenty-four hours. So how come they waited till I showed up to seek vengeance?"

Skagway Sam shot thoughtful glances at both the front and rear windows of the dinky pool hall before he said, "You sure come up with cheerful notions just as darkness is falling. They say Morgan Earp was blasted from outside in this very place, after dark. I suppose you know I was aiming to hustle you into a friendly little game of eight ball. But what say we call us even and move some place where we ain't such sitting ducks?"

Stringer said, "I've seen the Oriental, no offense, and I've other fish to fry. But just for the hell of it, have you ever heard of another newspaperman called Dutchy, here in Tombstone?"

Skagway Sam seemed sincere enough as he replied, "Can't say I have. But, then, me and Fran have only been here a few weeks, working with the new owners of the old Oriental."

As the two of them were putting their hats and coats back on, Skagway Sam shot another nervous glance at the black rear window and said, "Now, that's kind of spooky when you study on it. It was years and years ago, of course, but they do say Wyatt Earp once held my very same job at the Oriental. That was when the mines first opened and there was more money in town, dammit."

Stringer said, "I don't think any of the old-time gun-slicks want their jobs back. But just how tough have you

and your boys found it to keep things under control in the
Tombstone of here and now?"

Skagway Sam sighed. "You saw for yourself that poor
Knuckles, for one, hasn't *had* to prove himself before you
showed up. It gets a mite noisy when the cowhands are in
town. But to tell the pure and simple truth, that shoot-out
in the Tucson yards was the first serious fight I've been
mixed up in since we left Alaska. Man, you should have
seen the brawls we had up *there* on many a Saturday
night!"

Stringer said, "I did. I covered the gold rush for the
Sun. What there was of it. With the last big gold rush
petering out, a lot of rough ladies and gents besides you
and Miss Fran ought to be back in the States about now.
But . . . naw, that won't work."

Skagway Sam asked what wouldn't work, so Stringer
said, "A second boom, here in Tombstone. I heard how
you and your old pal, Soapy Smith, tried in vain to take
over Skagway, but . . ."

"Tried in vain, hell, we *took* it!" Skagway Sam cut in.

Stringer insisted, "Maybe so, for a while, at least. But
my point is that nobody fights all that hard to take over a
town that's half-empty and barely surviving on cowboy
weekends. This town just doesn't add up to a prize worth
killing for. At least, I don't *think* so. What if we're both
missing something? What if somebody thinks we're after
something, or out to write about something, that they know
about and we don't?"

Skagway Sam snorted in disgust. "There you go with
that vivid imagination again. Me and old Fran are in the
business of turning a quick profit. If there was anything left

more profitable than pushing liquor, cards, and pussy to dollar-a-day cowhands, do you really think we'd have missed it?"

Stringer didn't argue. They were out on the street again by this time, so they shook and parted friendly. But Stringer didn't turn his back on Skagway Sam until the rascal was out of range.

CHAPTER
SIX

It was an outside chance, but back in Frisco the *Sun* would still have its presses rolling and he knew old Sam Barca was a persistent cuss. So Stringer had another shot at the Western Union up the street and, sure enough, there was a wire from Barca waiting for him. It read, WIRE SERVICE DELETED BY WESTERN UNION UP STOP ORIGINAL MESSAGE READ FLOOD IN TOMBSTONE LODE NOT TOWN STOP SEE LOCAL RETIRED NEWSMAN FRED STEINMULLER FOR DETAILS STOP HOW ARE YOU COMING WITH OK CORRAL QUESTION MARK BARCA.

Stringer stuffed the telegram in a hip pocket in case he wound up with Steinmuller on the tip of his own tongue as well. Then he got out the card Annie Fraser had given him, asked directions to the address, and left, whistling "Roaming in the Gloaming."

Arizona Territory tried to make up for its torrid days

with its pleasantly balmy to downright cold nights. As he ambled away from the business center a big yellow moon was rising above the inky crests of the Dragoons to the east and somewhere a night-blooming jasmine was stinking almost too sweet. The side street he was following was narrower and unpaved, with picket fences, cactus hedges, or in some cases 'dobe walls screening the yards on either side. Despite the moonlight it seemed sort of spooky until he figured out what was wrong. There were hardly any lamps lit in the houses he passed and, this early in the evening, kids should have been playing kick the can or at least a few yard dogs should have been barking at him as he passed. It was silent as a graveyard. Tombstone might not be ghosted entire, yet. But it obviously took a lot fewer residents to run a half-shut-down business district than it had taken to work the silver mines up the slopes. In bonanza times there would have been lights along the hills over yonder, too. Mines worked around the clock, since it was twice as profitable and men working underground didn't care whether the sun or the moon might be shining, topside. It made him feel sort of sad to think of all the folk who'd lived here and all the kids who'd played here, just a few short years ago.

But he cheered up when he got to Annie's 'dobe and found she'd lit a light above her open door. As he crossed her tree-shaded yard he saw that the gal, herself, was sitting on a porch swing, off to one side in the shadows, as if she'd been expecting company.

As he joined her she patted the seat cushions at her side and said, "I was hoping you'd stop by. I remembered that old newspaperman's name just after you left."

He sat down beside her and put his hat aside as he asked

her if by any chance the name was Steinmuller. She clapped her hands with delight and replied, "That's right! Fred Steinmuller, better known as Dutchy. How did *you* know that?"

He said, "My boss just wired me to look him up. It seems he sends sort of murky leads to our wire service. To be fair, it might have been the work of a careless telegrapher. The old gent seems to have been talking about a flooded mine shaft. So tell me, miner's daughter, could a flooded mine shaft be considered *news?*"

"Hardly," she said. "The Dragoons are as full of water as silver. They had all the shafts on the pump by the time the veins pinched out. They'd have started to fill with ground water the day the last shift came out of the last pay dirt. Surely Dutchy should have known that."

"I reckon *I'd* have guessed as much, and I just got here. Do you reckon it's too late to pay a call on the old gent?" he asked.

She nodded. "It would be, by the time you could get to his place. He lives way up Turkey Creek Road, an hour or more on horseback. I naturally wrote his RFD down for you as soon as I remembered his name and looked his address up in our card index. You'd never find the place in the dark. Why don't you wait until morning?"

Stringer said he was willing. She said something in the Gaelic and leaped up to dash inside. He thought she was going to get the old man's address for him, but she sure seemed to take some time looking for it. It made more sense when she returned with coffee and marble cake. As she placed the tray on a bitty wrought-iron stand she hauled away from the 'dobe wall Stringer warned her, "You'd best go easy on the Gaelic around me. I only know a few phrases and the usual cuss words. A gal could get in trouble with me, trying to hold a conversation with me in the old lingo."

As she poured him a cup she sighed, saying, "Oh, dear, I was hoping to brush up on my Gaelic. You'd be surprised at how few Scots we have in these parts."

He said, "No I wouldn't. That's why I don't strain too hard to recall the songs my mother sang to me. My uncle Don MacKail has the Gaelic. Lord knows why. My dad always said that learning the Gaelic was a lot like learning to play the bagpipes. It takes a heap of study and, after you learn it, nobody wants to listen to you."

She asked, "Cream and sugar and don't you care about your heritage, Stuart?"

He shook his head, telling her, "I like it black and my heritage is native son. My grandfather was a forty-niner who found more grass than gold in the California hills. So he took to raising beef for the boys who panned for color and, in the end, I suspect he got more gold out of them there hills than they did. My elders used to jaw about the old country a lot, of course. My Uncle Don once accused a Mexican horse thief of being a Campbell. But, I dunno, most of the kids I grew up with in Calaveras County spoke plain American, Spanish, or Miwok. There's not much of a demand for fluency in Miwok, these days, either."

She sniffed primly and poured a cup for herself, lacing it with lots of cream and sugar, as she decided, "Maybe it's because both my parents left Inverness later. They sure missed the Highlands, to hear them talk when I was little. I mean to go there, one day. I've only seen pictures, but it looks so pretty."

He sipped some of his coffee. It was a little weak, but

he had no reason to stay up late, anyway. He said, "I talked to a California Irishman one time. Ireland's not all that far from Scotland, you know. Anyhow, he told me he'd saved up some money to go back and visit the town his people had been driven from and all by the Protestants and potatoes. He said once he got there he couldn't wait to get back. It was cold and clammy in high summer and the food was just awful."

He reached for a piece of marble cake, tasted it, and added, "This is swell. Even if it wasn't, it has to have *oatmeal* beat. That's all you get to eat in Scotland, save for maybe mutton or smoked herring, if you're rich. Sentiment's all right, up to a point, I reckon. But if our ancestors had found things all that grand in the old countries, they'd have never bothered to take *this* one away from the Indians."

She stared off into the distance as she allowed he might be right, from a purely practical sense. But then, sighing she said, "It's so dull and tedious here in Tombstone. Have you ever read *The Fair Maid of Perth,* by Sir Walter Scott? Life may have been hard in the old days of the Highland clans, but you have to admit things were more *romantic,* then."

He washed down some cake with black coffee before he told her, "I doubt it. Old Walter Scott was a lowlander, writing long after the Battle of the North Inch, in the comfort of his snug and dry study. He never had to traipse around barefoot in wet heather with soggy and likely stinky kilts over his goose bumps. As for that battle in that book, Scott got the facts all wrong. That fight was between two different clans entire."

He brightened, adding, "You know what? Those early

Victorian novels about the deadly doings of the Highland clans were a heap like what's been happening here more *recent*. A lot of folk who were there are still alive, and they're already making up a mess of myths about recently dead or still living gunslicks. My fool feature editor wants me to write up a whopper about the gunfight at the O.K. Corral because a gunfight in a vacant lot sounds sort of silly. I'm tempted just to cite old Wyatt's official version and let it go at that. Lord knows we could both use the money."

She didn't seem interested in anything that had ever taken place in Tombstone. She'd put her cup and saucer down to just lean back in the swing, languorously, as she murmured, sort of teasingly, *"Och, pugga mi agus pugga mi gu math."*

He put down his own cup, took her in his arms, and kissed her as good as he knew how. She struggled at first, then kissed him back the same way. But when they came up for air she giggled, red-faced, and said, "I thought you said you didn't have the Gaelic."

He went on holding her, but his voice was stern as he replied, "I *told* you a gal could get in trouble with me, that way. If you didn't want me to kiss you, why did you ask me to?"

She fluttered her lashes and answered in a small confused tone, "I was just having fun with you. I mean, I didn't think you'd understand and, even if you did, you should have understood I was just making *fun* of you."

He said, "I'd rather you had fun *with* me than *of* me," and kissed her some more. He felt pretty sure they were both having fun.

But she twisted her lips from his and pleaded, weakly,

"Oh, don't. Please don't. You're making me feel so wicked and . . ." Then she sighed. "My late mother warned me about you Lochaber men." Then she kissed him instead of waiting to be kissed. But when he unpinned her hair she gasped, "I *beg* your pardon, sir! Just what do you think you're doing?"

He let go of her and said, soberly, "You're right. I'd best go back to the Cosmopolitan and see if they ever found me a new mattress."

She blinked at him in the soft light. "I give up. Don't they usually provide proper hotel beds in a hotel?"

"Sure. Only this afternoon someone blew the one I had all to feather fluff with dynamite. I wasn't in it, of course. So they may have just been funning. If worse comes to worst I can always find me another place to bunk. So could I have Fred Steinmuller's address, now?"

She sat up straighter, her unpinned auburn hair spilling down to the porch swing seat as he'd suspected it might. "I'll get it, if you simply can't stand my company another minute," she sulked.

He smiled knowingly at her and replied, "You know all too well how much I enjoy your company and mayhaps vice versa. But there's no sense getting all worked up over nothing, so—"

"Are you calling me a nothing?" she cut in, eyes blazing out of focus without her specs to guide them.

He said, soothingly, "Of course you ain't a nothing. You're a high-toned lady librarian and I don't even have a library card."

Eyebrow raised, she demanded, "Oh? And I suppose that means you think I'm just a silly little bookworm whose only experience with lovemaking comes from *reading* about it?"

He chuckled wearily. "Hold your fire. I surrender unconditional. I never meant to imply you kissed like a book, Miss Annie."

She said, "You'd better not! I guess I know who's small-town and who isn't, around here!" Then she kissed him again, harder than before, and when she added a French accent to her kissing it seemed only natural for him to fondle her more intimately as they set the swing to swaying on its chains. But, just as he was beginning to wonder how far one could go on a porch swing, assuming it was possible, she gasped, "Not out here, you fool!" So he picked her up in his arms and headed for the open door with her as she grinned up at him like a kid swiping apples to ask, "Do you still think I'm just a simple country girl?"

As he carried her inside and paused to get his bearings, he told her, "I don't know what you might be, save for being beautiful, but I can't wait to find out!"

She said, "Neither can I. It's the doorway to the left of the fireplace, darling!"

He carried her through it and, sure enough, found a big old four-poster to lower her down to. As he dropped atop her to kiss her some more she giggled and said, "*Now* you're sorry you're not wearing kilts, I'll bet. Get out of those jeans this instant and get rid of your spurs and gun belt while you're at it. I can manage this summer dress without your help."

She sure could, he saw, as she beat him at stripping, easily, and lay back naked and expectantly atop the counterpane in the spreading auburn mist of her long hair. There was just enough soft lamplight through her open bedroom doorway to create a vision of loveliness without having to worry about any warts or wrinkles she might have had. As he lowered his own nude body against hers it hardly seemed likely there was a single blemish on her soft creamy skin. As he entered her she gasped in mingled desire and surprise. Then with a contented sigh she said, "I knew I was waiting for a Highland laddy!" and proceeded to prove by her pelvic gyrations that she was either making that up, or that one hell of a lot of Scotsmen had passed through Tombstone in her time.

He didn't make any rude comments, later, when she felt it was time to sob about losing her fool head and that she'd just never, never—or hardly ever—did this sort of thing with any other man she'd barely met. That was the trouble with librarians. They read too many romantic novels, where hardly anyone got to screw just for pleasure. When she asked if he'd respect her in the morning he was sport enough to allow he surely would and that inspired her to get on top. She sure looked pretty up there, with her long auburn hair flying all over the place as her perky breasts bounced up and down. Then he rolled her over to finish right, with an elbow hooked under both of her knees, and she said it made her feel grand to be treated so romantic, even if this was all his fault.

Nothing that good could last forever, or even as long as he wanted it to. So the time came for Stringer to roll a smoke and share it with her while their bodies dried and they fought for their second winds. She was a sport about smoking Bull Durham. But it got sort of tedious to hear her go on and on about the way he'd taken advantage of her weak nature. So he told her he loved her in the Gaelic, figuring that wouldn't prey on his conscience as much when the time came to move on.

That prompted her to cuddle closer, but, as if she'd read his mind, she sighed and said, "That's easy enough to say, at times like these. But what happens when it's time for you to go back to San Francisco, Stuart?"

He shrugged. "At the rate I'm going, I'll be stuck here indefinite. If I don't watch my step, I may wind up here *permanent*. By the way, is that Boot Hill tale about Tombstone for real?"

It worked. It got her off the subject of his leaving as she told him, "Of course not. Naturally there's a potter's field for dead paupers, but would you like to be the undertaker who had to tell someone like Old Man Clanton that his dear dead son, Billy, wasn't good enough to be buried among gentlefolk?"

"That's what I thought. Who do you reckon put up those plaques, pointing out all sorts of local wonders that never was?"

She yawned and snuggled closer. "The local chamber of commerce, of course. We were starting to get a lot of curious visitors before they shut down the rail spur. Some cross-country travelers just don't seem to think they've crossed the country if they can't say they saw the Grand Canyon or at least the O.K. Corral."

As he snuffed out their smoke he mused, half to himself, "Some folk sure are funny. The first time I was through Cheyenne they were arguing a bond issue to pave the streets, put in electric lights, and raise the town to modern standards or more so. But the last time I was there, covering their big rodeo, they were holding covered-wagon races in the streets and all the drug store clerks in town were clanging spurs, spitting tobacco, and shooting up streetlamps."

She didn't answer. She was asleep, which was only fair, when one considered all the exercise they'd just indulged in.

He lay his head back and closed his own eyes. But sleep just wouldn't come. It was one thing to doze off after a day well spent in a library, with nothing to worry about worse than folk bringing books in late. It was another thing entire to sleep the sleep of the just when someone seemed out to kill you, and you had no idea who it might be, or why.

Miss Annie had been right about one thing. He'd have never been able to find old Fred Steinmuller's place in the dark. Even as Stringer rode Blue Ribbon up the Turkey Creek Road in the crisp morning light he was beginning to think he'd been given the wrong directions. The gravel stream bed to his left as he rode along one rut of the wagon trace looked more like a dry wash than a creek, and if there were any turkeys about they were living on mesquite and cheat grass. He could see by bigger tree stumps up the slopes to either side that there'd been a time when these hills had been timbered with juniper and oak, both of which provided mast in the form of nuts and seeds. But the timber had been cut for mine props and no doubt many a turkey had wound up in a miner's pot. Semiarid hill country took a long time to recover, even when left alone by man. The opportunistic mesquite had made it back to high chaparral, and cheat grass would grow in pavement cracks if you didn't watch out. But it would be many a year, even with the silver mines abandoned, before there'd be timber worth cutting in these parts again.

The trail wound around a big clump of prickly pear, eight to ten feet high, and then, even before he could see where all the noise was coming from, a mule was bawling its fool head off at Stringer or, more likely, his pony.

They moved on up the trail. He spied a rusty corrugated tin roof above walls of whitewashed 'dobe. The unhappy mule was in a pole corral out back. Stringer could see at a glance it was in bad shape. A horse would have been dead by now. The poor brute had been surviving on pear pads until it had eaten all the cactus it could get at over the top rail of the corral. Stringer called out, "Hello the house! Is anybody home and, if so, can't you see your critter needs watering?"

There was no answer. Stringer spurred Blue Ribbon forward, around to the back, and dismounted to climb through the corral poles and get at the rusty hand pump by the dry and empty water trough. The mule already had its thirsty muzzle down in the rust and dust of the trough. Springer worked the pump handle and got nothing but an excuse to curse as the dried-out leather valves brought up nothing but Arizona air. He rolled back through the corral poles as the poor mule brayed and tried to follow him. He got a canteen from his saddle and got back to the pump as fast as he could. The fool mule tried to bite the canteen and the hand holding it away from Stringer. He punched its muzzle away and poured half the contents in the trough. As the mule tried to wet its whistle with the little that didn't soak right into the crud, Stringer primed the pump with what was left in the canteen. It took a full minute for the leather gasket and flutter valve to soften and swell. By then the mule was arguing with him about the now-empty canteen again. But that was soon put to rights by the sputtering stream of pump water. As the trough began to fill, old Blue Ribbon forgot her vaquero training and dragged her grounded reins over to stick her own head through the corral poles and help the mule drink all the water in sight. Stringer pumped until he felt sure there was enough for both, albeit not too much; then he left the two brutes there and went off to find out why on earth the mule's owner treated livestock so disgusting.

As he opened the back door of the one-room 'dobe, gun drawn, he forgave the old man stretched out on a corner bunk. From the color of his shrunken face, and the way it smelled in here, it seemed obvious he'd been dead some time. The exact time was hard to judge in such dry country. Folk tended to dry up and mummify if left where the birds and bugs couldn't get at them. Stringer left the back door wide, then opened the front door and all the windows. It helped, some, but he knew that if he shut the damper on the potbellied stove in one corner, and let some newsprint sort of smolder, he'd feel better about breathing and thus might be able to stay in here long enough to figure out what had happened.

But as he moved to what he'd taken at first to be bales of old newspaper aboard a packing box in another corner, he saw that while some of the paper had gone buttered-toast brown with age, the stacks were neatly divided with pasteboard markers. Some had been bound like notebooks with brown butcher's paper, and some few darker-brown bundles, deeper in the piles, were in fact actual scrap-books, with old newspaper clippings pasted neatly to their now-dry-and-crumbling manila pages. Stringer ignored the odor of dry death—it was fading some by now in any case—and scouted an old army garrison trunk at the foot of the dead man's bunk. He only had to see a few old mail envelopes to know who he was talking to as he told the wrinkled corpse, "I'm sure sorry about this, Dutchy Steinmuller. I wanted to talk to you about a heap of things and now you can't even tell me why you're dead."

He moved closer to the old man's partly mummified face. The yellowed teeth were bared in a ghastly grin and the eye sockets stared back at him with what looked like a pair of dried prunes. The body wasn't mummified enough to move without stinking the whole place up again, and in any case Stringer was hardly qualified as a medical examiner. It was no doubt wiser to let the county figure out how old Steinmuller had died. Meanwhile, Sam Barca, back in Frisco, still wanted to know whatever could have possessed the old-timer to dispatch a news lead that made little or no sense.

As Stringer rolled a smoke, staring about at his humble surroundings, he found it less mysterious. The wire services paid just enough for tips to make sending them in worthwhile. The old ex-newspaperman would have known that, and the two to five dollars the wire service had paid him, if it had paid him yet, would have been big money to anyone living this close to the bone. Stringer went back to paw through the contents of the trunk. There was only the mail in the lift-out drawer atop a mess of old clothes. He didn't find any envelopes addressed to the old man from any wire service. That was easily explained by the simple fact that they paid at the end of the month. But it asked another question. There should have been a mess of payments from more than one wire service if the old-timer had been one of those fool pests who sent in tales of two-headed calves and haunted houses. Ergo, old Steinmuller had considered his tip real news. But news about what? There was nothing new about abandoned mine shafts filling up with ground water. The pump out back had just proven the water table wasn't half that deep in these parts.

Stringer lit the smoke he'd built and told the dead man, "I'd best carry your mule and the news of your demise back to town and let them tidy up whatever needs to be tidied. Sam Barca won't be able to say I never tried."

But he decided, as long as he was there, he'd have a look-see through those carefully saved old newspapers. He hoped to find a few items of interest. What he found was a gold mine. The old-timer had not only saved back issues of all four Tombstone papers, he'd indexed them by date of publication and pasted up separate scrapbooks dealing with ongoing items of local interest. A lot of back issues were missing, of course. Stringer could see at a glance the old man hadn't tried to store twenty years' worth of back issues. None of the papers kept simply as papers had been cut up with scissors. It was safe to assume the old man had put anything left over from his scrapbook building into that old stove. Nine out of ten issues of any paper published in a small town wouldn't have been worth saving to begin with. But, as it was, there was a quarter ton of moldering newsprint here. So Stringer simply dug out the dozen or so scrapbooks, figuring they'd be the cream of the old man's collection. They still made quite a load. But he was sore put to decide which, if any, he'd want to leave behind. Old Steinmuller had collected a heavy tome on the Earp family, another on the Clantons and their pal, old Sheriff John Behan. Some of the thinner volumes seemed to detail the deadly doings of lesser mortals like Curly Bill and Johnny Ringo. But the old-timer had been interested in the politics and economics of the mining town as well. Stringer hauled his trove out in two loads and lashed them with latigo leather to ride like saddlebags behind him. Then he closed all the doors and windows the way he'd found them, to keep critters out, and let the mule out of the corral before he mounted up to ride back to town.

The muled followed like a pup for about a mile. Then all of a sudden it wasn't back there anymore. Stringer didn't worry about it. He knew mules, ponies, and, hell, some said camels the army had experimented with out here before the Civil War, could get along on their own in these parts. How they managed was their own problem.

Knowing where he was and where he was going, it seemed to take him far less time to get back to Tombstone. It was just as well. It was warming up again by the time he made the city limits. He stopped first at the library and lugged his two bundles of scrapbooks in to show Annie. He found her fussing at a pair of dirty-faced little boys about the condition they'd returned a picture book in. She seemed less than thrilled to see Stringer, even after she'd gotten rid of the kids. She said, "Darling, you're going to have to quit pestering me night and day. People are bound to talk."

"I didn't come to pester you," he protested. "I want to leave these scrapbooks here with you for safekeeping. I got them out at Steinmuller's place. I found him dead. So now I have to report that to the law."

She gasped, "How dreadful! But isn't the law likely to consider anything you took from out there evidence, or at least part of his estate?"

Stringer said, "That's why I don't want 'em on me when I stop by the marshal's office. The law's likely to impound everything from his water pump to his socks and just store 'em all some place and forget 'em. I want to read through the old-timer's collected wisdom as soon as I have the time. I figure as long as my feature editor wants yet another version of the deadly doings in old-time Tombstone it's about time somebody got things right. Thanks to old Steinmuller's saving ways, it ought to be a snap."

She looked away. "I don't know, Stuart," she murmured. "You know how I feel about you, but I'm not sure I want to get mixed up in anything that might be against the law."

"That'll learn me to tell the truth to a woman. Don't worry. I was dumb to ask and they'll likely be just as safe at my hotel."

She nodded, but then she shot him a thoughtful look. "Oh? Were you planning on staying there, later this evening?"

He shot a thoughtful look back at her as he replied, "I got to stay somewhere till Knuckles Ashton makes up his mind whether to live or die. Your move, Annie."

She hesitated before she said, "My head's telling me one thing, in the clear light of daytime. I know what other parts of me are sure to feel like, after dark, if we quit while we're ahead. So, yes, I want you to come by my place, later tonight, but can I trust you to be discreet, dear? The neighbors, you know."

He chuckled fondly. "If I'm checked into the Cosmopolitan, official, and don't come calling on you with a brass band, we might not wreck your rep entire."

But as he picked up the bundles of scrapbooks he

added, in a more sober tone, "Don't count on me showing up early, if then. I might wind up in jail, or worse, between now and then."

She gasped, "Oh, heavens, maybe you'd best not tell anyone anything about what you found out at Dutchy Steinmuller's."

He said, "I got to. It's one thing to bend the law a mite. It's another to bust it entire. I doubt I'll have any trouble when I report the old gent's death. If I'm not at your place by, say, ten or eleven, feel free to start without me."

She laughed and called him a big goof. By the time he'd ridden on to his hotel, scrapbooks and all, he was beginning to agree with her. Men as well as women thought more sensible in the daytime, and how on earth was he supposed to whip up that Sunday feature for the *Sun* if the horny but cautious gal wouldn't allow him to darken her door with Steinmuller's scrapbooks?

When he got to the Cosmopolitan he stabled Blue Ribbon and lugged the two bundles in through a side entrance. The clerk on duty seemed surprised to see him again. He told Stringer, "We have your bag here, under the desk. When you didn't come back last night we assumed you'd checked out."

Stringer growled, "I'd have come back to get my possibles and settle up if I was leaving town. I sure hope you've cleaned up the same room? It saves asking for a new key."

The clerk seemed a mite dubious. He went back to get the hotel manager, a priss who fussed at Stringer about his uncouth habits until Stringer told him to stop fussing and figure the damages. Then they got to be pals again. The manager said the blown-out windowpanes had cost eight dollars to replace and that while the bedstead, being brass, had survived the blast, the extra bedding and mattress added up to another ten bucks. Stringer handed over a double eagle and demanded a receipt with his change. There was an outside chance his paper would allow the outlay as legitimate travel expenses. He could just see the bookkeeper's face when she got to the part about dynamite.

Having squared accounts with the Cosmopolitan, and enlisted two bits' worth of assistance from a bellhop, Stringer got all his stuff back up to the same room and stored the scrapbooks in the closet atop his gladstone. The new bedding looked a mite used, and they'd missed a few feathers in the corners, but what the hell. He locked up again and went back down to get the harder chore over with.

CHAPTER
SEVEN

He found Wes Rhodes in his office, gnawing a ham on rye, and told the town law he'd found old Dutchy Steinmuller dead.

Rhodes put down his sandwich with a sigh. "Curly Bill and Buckskin Frank were before my time, here. But you sure seem out to become a legend in your own right, MacKail. What makes you so unsafe to be around? You don't *look* all that dangerous."

Stringer snorted in disgust. "Hell, I never said I'd killed the old man. I just said I found him dead. I don't know how he got in that unpleasant condition. But all you have to do is look at him to see he's been dead some time. I just got here; Steinmuller's been dead since before I arrived and all the time since."

Rhodes wiped some grease from his mouth, his eyes staring thoughtfully up at Stringer. Then he shrugged. "Or so you say," he said. "Where'd you find the old man, MacKail?"

Stringer said, "In bed, at home, out on Turkey Creek Road. He was too shriveled up for me to guess whether he died on his own or with somebody's help. He was lying there natural. There was no sign of a struggle, and a mule worth stealing was still out back."

Rhodes decided, "I'll send some boys out there with a buckboard, a tarp, and some quicklime. I know where it is. I also know old Dutchy was seventy if he was a day and wouldn't have put up enough of a struggle to matter. You still at the Cosmopolitan, MacKail?"

Stringer said, "I'm still checked in there, if that's what you mean."

"That's just what I mean," Rhodes confirmed. "If someone's dead, total, I'm going to have to wire the sheriff down in Bisbee about it. Whether he wants to let you wander about loose until we can figure out why so many folk get hurt around you or not is up to him."

"My conscience is clean as a whistle as far as that old man I never met, alive, is concerned," Stringer vowed. "I take it from your tolerant attitude that Knuckles Ashton is still with us, alive and well?"

Rhodes said, "I can't say how alive and well he might feel, right now. I know he ain't with us. One of the fancy gals attending to him found his bed empty this very morning. We've asked around town. Nobody's seen hide nor hair of him, since. I don't suppose you'd know where he might have gone, MacKail?"

"I didn't know he'd even got up, until just now. Maybe he just felt mortified and rode out of town on his own."

"With a bullet wound in his ass?" asked the town law,

dubiously, before demanding, "By the way. They say you didn't spend the night at your hotel last night, either. I don't suppose you'd want to say where you was when the gent you shot, more than once, sort of vanished off the face of the earth?"

"I can't," Stringer said. "Since I assume you to be a man of the world, I reckon I can ask you what you'd think of a man who'd ask a lady he's not married up with to alibi him."

Wes Rhodes raised an eyebrow. "In my opinion, a man who'd kiss and tell would eat shit off a shovel. On the other hand, that's a mighty time-worn excuse and you're better known in Tombstone as a gunfighter than a lover."

Stringer smiled thinly. "That's the first good news I've had all morning. Am I free to go, Wes?"

The town law said, "I'm still thinking about that." Then they both blinked in surprise as a railroad whistle moaned loudly close by. Wes Rhodes got to his feet, muttering, "What the hell?" as he headed for the door. Then he added, "You better tag along, MacKail. I'll figure out what to do about you once I figure out why there seems to be a railroad engine somewhere in town."

The two of them stepped out in the harsh sunlight. They could both tell by the others running that way, even before they spied the pillar of smoke above the closed-down Tombstone depot, that a train had indeed steamed up from the main line along the out-of-service spur.

As Stringer and Wes Rhodes joined the puzzled throng down the street a parade of curious-looking dudes marched out of the depot, squinting around in the bright sunlight as if they'd all just arrived in a mighty exotic part of the world. From the way some of them were dressed, they had. Wes Rhodes muttered, "I give up. The opera house is closed and none of them look like sopranos to begin with." Then he spotted someone he knew in the crowd and moved over to demand, "What's going on, here, Lawyer Lumford?"

The local lawyer, if that was what he was, struck Stringer as a jolly fat man in a seersucker suit and straw skimmer. His sensible riding boots saved him from looking as greenhorn as the others in his party. He smiled at the town law and said, "Pilgrims to the Promised Land, Wes. Investors, anyways. We just got the S.P. to run us a special over from L.A. so's these gents could have a look at the Lucky Cuss."

Wes Rhodes frowned. "How come? That vein pinched out no later than '99 and it's full of water besides."

Lawyer Lumford looked smug as he replied, "A lot you know. A syndicate has been formed to open the mine again. They might open *all* the shafts again if the Lucky Cuss pans out." He shot a friendly glance at Stringer. "I don't believe I know this young gent, Wes."

The town law said, "He's a murder suspect. His name's MacKail. What are you trying to pull on these poor dudes, Lawyer Lumford? If there was two bits' worth of silver left in them hills they'd have never pulled up stakes and abandoned every shaft, owing a lot of bills here in town."

The portly lawyer insisted, "The old-timers weren't scientific. They gave up when the ore got harder to produce, not when it was all gone."

Stringer asked, "Isn't that the same thing?"

Lumford replied, expansively, "Not at all, son. Modern machinery can keep the shafts dry, a lot cheaper as well as better than the old steam pumps. Modern extraction methods can leach bullion from ore too low grade for the old-time gut-and-gitters to mess with. The big bonanza days may be over. Gone are the days when a drifter with a miner's pan could get rich, easy. But even if the cream's been skimmed, there's still a lot of silver and, who knows, even gold in them there hills."

Wes Rhodes looked disgusted. "You've been out in the sun too long, Lawyer Lumford," he decided. "In the best of times there was never no gold in the Dragoons."

Some of his dudes were drifting over, looking lost. Lumford told Rhodes, "Don't worry yourself about it, Wes. Nobody's asking you to buy any mining shares, you know."

Then he waved his straw skimmer at his dudes and said, "This way, gents. First we'll get you checked into the Hardwood or Cosmopolitan. Then we'll all go over to the O.K. Corral and you can have your pictures taken right on the scene of the famous gunfight!"

They all seemed to feel that was a grand notion. As the promoter led his gaggle of thirty-odd geese on down the street, the town law spat. "Shit," he muttered, "they'll find more silver in the O.K. Corral than down the flooded shaft of the Lucky Cuss. Drunken cowhands are always dropping loose change as they mount up. Them miners left the mountain cold sober as well as disgusted."

Stringer said, soberly, "I wasn't there. Did you know Dutchy Steinmuller sent out a garbled report about flooding in the Tombstone Lode, not too long before he died, one way or another, or that my own troubles began when I was sent by my paper to sort that out?"

Wes Rhodes said, "We'll let the county coroner decide what killed the old man. If you're suggesting he was done in to keep him from telling the outside world them shafts was full of water, or that someone's been trying to keep you from reporting the same, the two of you must have been drinking from the same bottle. Make that the three of you if we throw in that fool lawyer. The goddam mines have been flooded since they was abandoned. Everybody knows that. So where the hell is there a mystery worth shooting a crow over?"

Stringer said, "I don't know. I'm still working on it. Am I under arrest, Wes?"

Rhodes said, "Naw, just try to stay out of any more trouble. I got to make sure them poor dudes don't get in trouble, now. You know how some of the boys can act when they spy patent shoes and sissy spats." He started to stride after the parade. Then he turned to shout back, "Don't you go leaving town before I tell you you can, hear?"

Stringer raised his own voice to protest, "Dammit, Wes. If Knuckles Ashton can leave town, why can't I?"

"We don't know where Knuckles might be, dead or alive, and the coroner just might want to talk to you about old Dutch Steinmuller, depending on how the autopsy turns out. That'll be down in Bisbee and even with the train running, if it's still running, that's sure to take some time." Then he turned and walked faster to catch up with Lawyer Lumford and his dudes.

Stringer swore and might have followed at a less tiring pace had not a buckboard loaded with baggage cut him off as it tore around one end of the depot. He'd just finished cursing that when a more interesting box wagon came out the same slot with a cargo of red fifty-gallon fuel drums. Stringer trotted along beside to ask the driver how come.

The driver reined his mule team to a politer pace as he called down, "Gasoline, they call it. It's sort of like naphtha."

Stringer replied, "I know what gasoline is. A few folk in my part of Frisco drive horseless carraiges. I meant how come they want so much of the stuff here in Tombstone. No offense, but I've yet to see any gas buggies in this town."

The teamster answered, friendly enough, "None taken. There ain't none. This load is for the thumping wonder up to the Lucky Cuss. They got a bodacious internally combusticated water pump up yonder. It come all the way from France to pump out the old mine, see?"

Stringer didn't see, but it was too hot to keep dogtrotting down the middle of the dusty street, so he waved the wagon a polite *adios* and veered off to do something more sensible. Since it was going on noon now, the most sensible notion he could come up with involved fried eggs on a bed of chili con carne, washed down with iced Coca-Cola, at a stand-up greasy spoon on the shady side of the street.

After that, since he was already in the neighborhood, he headed for the Western Union office to see if they could help him make a lick of sense out of Dutchy Steinmuller's inane report that long-flooded mine shafts were flooded.

They couldn't. The clerk out front was friendly enough to call his telegrapher from the back, seeing business was slow at that time of the day in any case. They both recalled Dutchy Steinmuller coming in to send a wire, at urgent day rates, any number of days ago. The old man didn't come into town much anymore and, when he did, he seldom spent on a nickel-a-word telegram.

Stringer asked if they kept written records of such transactions. The counterman looked startled as he replied, "Lord have mercy, have you any idea how many messages we send each week? When a customer writes his message on a blank, out here, I carry it in to Jake, and it goes out within the hour."

Jake said, "I stick it on a spike and type it up on the tape machine. By the time the night man comes on duty there's usually a dozen or more spiked atop it. When the spike can't hold no more we pull everything off and start all over. We keep the original mayhaps one day, in case anyone accuses us of a mistake. Then it all goes in the trash barrel or the stove, depending on the time of the year."

Stringer nodded as that sank in. Then he asked, "Can I take it you and the other wire services send typed messages instead of the old dots and dashes, these days?"

"The railroads still use Morse, the cheap bastards," Jake sneered. "Edison's ticker tape's a lot faster and sends fewer mistakes. They say that some other inventor back East is working on an electricated typewriter that will type regular pages at a distance. I sure would like that. As she is, we got to pull the tape out of the ticker, cut it to size, and paste it on the telegram blank."

"You don't save any of such ticker tape, even in, say, a waste basket?" Stringer asked hopefully.

The two Western Union men exchanged blank stares. Then Jake said, "I follow your drift. But you're sniffing the wrong pole. The ticker only feeds us one copy on tape and naturally the customer gets that. As for messages sent *out* of here, as in the case you're asking about, we never *see* the damned tape. It comes off the spool at the other end."

Stringer started to ask a dumb question before he

thought harder and muttered, "Right. If you'd sent a garbled message from here, by accident, my boss in Frisco
wouldn't have been able to get the wire service to admit
they'd been the ones who sent the report that the town
rather than the lode of Tombstone had been flooded just
awful. But, whether Steinmuller's tip was sent one way or
the other, what could the old gent have had in mind?"

The counterman shrugged, suggesting, "He was old and
sort of dotty, even when he was sober, which was seldom.
They say he hardly ever left his 'dobe up in the hills. He
was working on some kind of collection, butterflies or
more likely stamps. What if he just got restless one day,
wandered on up to the old digging on his old mule, and
noticed for the first time that the shafts were flooded.
Might not that have struck a crazy old hermit as fresh
news?"

"I wish that didn't work so good. It explains the fool's
errand I was sent on better than it does that dynamite in my
bed," Stringer hated to admit.

Jake said, "We heard. Wes Rhodes keeps wiring the
county all about you. We heard that just before you got to
Tombstone you saved Skagway Sam's life, too. Him and
that painted whore of his are about as popular in these parts
as the pox half their soiled doves are said to carry. You
might have just made somebody mad at you for preventing
rough justice."

"I've talked to Skagway about that. Nobody's tried to
kill *him* since he and Faro Fran came back from L.A.,"
Stringer retorted.

Jake said, "Trying to take out Skagway Sam, here in
Tombstone where he owns a private army, could take years
off a man's life. It was hard enough to ambush him in

Tucson, where his backbone wasn't supposed to be so well guarded." He shrugged. "Maybe someone figures that if they can't make a meal of Skagway Sam, they can at least take a bite of you, his old pal."

Snorting in disgust, Stringer protested, "That's just plain dumb. I'm not friends with that bunch at the Oriental Saloon. I may have saved them in Tucson from a back-shooting, which was only Christian. But I'd no sooner arrived in Tombstone than I had to shoot it out with one of Skagway Sam's bully boys."

The counterman said, soothingly, "Hell, nobody *here* ever said you was tied in with that disgusting bunch. We just suggested that somebody else who hates 'em more ferocious might not think as clear and logical, see?"

Stringer said, "Sort of. They'd have to be disgusting indeed to drive anyone that *loco en la cabeza.*"

"They surely are disgusting," Jake said knowingly. "It ain't the way it was when good old Lou Rickabaugh was running vice on Allen Street. Before Sheriff Slaughter got elected on a nice-nelly reform platform and ran just about all the old sporting crowd out of the territory, a man could play an honest game of chance or get laid without winding up crippled for life. With Rickabaugh gone and the sheriff's department moved clean down to Bisbee, you can't hope to win at cards and you may as well take sheep shears to your poor old dong as shove it in one of Faro Fran's whores."

Stringer thanked him for the warning and left, little wiser than before. The sun was really bearing down, now, and the town law had told him to stay out of trouble. So he went back to his hotel, had a quick bath, and locked himself in, naked, with the old scrapbooks he'd brought back from Steinmuller's place. He spread the ones covering the Earps and Clantons on the bed and got out his own notepad as he leafed through the moldering pages, taking occasional notes in shorthand as he tried to patch together a sensible Sunday feature.

It wasn't easy. Clippings from the *Epitaph* or *Nugget,* covering the same events, read just the opposite. To the *Nugget*'s way of thinking the Earps were city slickers, horse thieves, pimps, and worse yet, Damnyankees.

The *Epitaph,* published by New Yorker John Clum, took the position that even the Earps' somewhat sinister pal, Doc Holliday, was an amusing rogue who doubtless meant well, while the Clantons and their friends were Texas trash who raped cows, stole Mexicans, and cussed in front of ladies. The two less partisan papers gave both factions mixed reviews. Neither side seemed all good or all bad to the *Expositor* or *Evening Gossip,* but they seldom agreed on all the details, either.

Stringer had the advantage that he'd met the likeable compulsive talker, Wyatt Earp, and his lovely but loony young wife, Josephine Sara Marcus, when they'd been running a saloon in the Alaska gold fields, long after the events so scrambled in all the old newspaper clippings on top of his bed. He knew the truth just wasn't in old Earp if it got in the way of a good yarn, while his young wife, who'd never been there, dreamed up real whoppers her doting husband was too polite to correct. It was thanks to her romantic imagination—and no doubt the imagination of her she-male rivals—that some said Wyatt had courted her away from his enemy, Sheriff Behan, while others recalled her as the notorious Tombstone Sadie, a slut that might have made Messalina blanch.

Stringer had already known, and the old clippings confirmed, that at the time his present wife was still in pigtails both Earp and Sheriff Behan had been attached to other ladies in Tombstone. As a man who knew his way around San Francisco, Stringer felt inclined to go along with old Wyatt's boast that he'd lured his present pretty baby from the wicked stage, where she'd been performing as a Frisco entertainer noted more for her looks than her talent. The less-glamorous seamstress he'd been living with in his Tombstone days had been called Mattie. The *Epitaph* had her down as a seamstress of note and Wyatt's third wife. The *Nugget* took the position that she'd been a local whore old Wyatt had lived with on and off without formal ceremony. Either way, she'd been left behind when the Earps moved on, sudden, and she'd died soon after from strong drink or by her own hand, depending on which paper was publishing her pitiful obituary.

The two more objective papers as well as the *Nugget* cast considerable doubt on old Wyatt's current brag about his shoot-out with Curly Bill Brocius, alias Graham, by reporting Curly Bill alive and obnoxious as ever ten years after Earp claimed he shot him at Iron Springs. There apparently had been *some* sort of fuss over yonder, because there were several clippings detailing the efforts of Arizona Territory to have Doc Holliday arrested up in Colorado for the murder of one Florentino Cruz, who'd been either a ferocious cow thief or an innocent Mexican-American cowhand, depending on whether one read of his demise in the *Epitaph* or the *Nugget*. The case had been dropped when Holliday checked into a Glenwood Springs sanitarium to cough the last of his lungs out and die with his boots off.

By the time Stringer finished putting his notes in order it was just too damned hot to start his Sunday feature, so he put the project aside and just lay down to die for a spell.

After a short, sweaty nap and a longer second soak in the bath down the hall, Stringer decided it couldn't be any hotter outside than in and got dressed again. Strapping on his six-gun, he locked up and went down to the tap room. Nobody was there but the barkeep and Wes Rhodes, sipping a lonesome rum and tonic. Stringer bellied up to the bar beside the town law and told the barkeep he'd try the same, with less rum and more ice. Then he asked Rhodes, "Do you drink here often or were you worried about my leaving town?"

Rhodes smiled thinly. "You're the least of my worries, old son. I saw what the boys hauled back from Steinmuller's place. It couldn't have been you. You ain't been here that long."

"I noticed," Stringer replied, smiling back. "He'd have been in worse shape if you enjoyed more humidity in these parts."

Rhodes grimaced. "He was only dried out on top. When the boys tried to pick him up, most of him came up stiff as a plank. But a lot of him stayed on the bedding, more sticky. They brung the bedding and the goo in as well, of course. It's a good thing they did. The county coroner never would have noticed that rifle ball if the boys had left it behind."

The barkeep slid Stringer's highball across the mahogany to him. Stringer picked it up with a nod of thanks and asked the town law what rifle ball they were talking about.

Rhodes said, "A .30-caliber deer or military slug, copper clad. From where it was stuck to the bedspread with a gob of old Dutch Steinmuller, we figure he was hit low in the back at long range. It must have smarted some, but the tough old buzzard made it on home and just lay down to get over it or not. Anyone can see he didn't get over it. The poor old fool should have come on into town. It wouldn't have been a fatal wound if he hadn't treated it so casual."

Stringer sipped some cool bitter blandness. He'd said easy on the rum, not no rum at all, but mayhaps it was just as well on such a hot day. He put the cold clammy glass back down and told Rhodes, "Try it this way. He was afraid to ride into town once he'd made it home and felt more forted up. I was wondering how his mule survived so long, out back, even with cactus to get at. What if he lasted a while with that slug in him? What if he sort of agreed with you that it was only a flesh wound from a spent bullet? He might have pumped the watering trough full to the brim and done some other chores before it came to him that he was feeling poorly and lay down to die, see?"

Rhodes frowned down at his own drink as he replied, "Only partway. I follow you as far as making sure his mule would be all right for a spell. The front door was barred from the inside. The back door wasn't. My boys agreed with you that there was nothing out of order in the 'dobe, save for him. So what other chores could you have in mind for a dying man to tend to?"

Stringer explained, "He could have burnt any number of papers in his potbellied stove and it would still have been cold by the time I showed up. I took the liberty of looking about for some papers he should have had out there. I didn't find them."

Rhodes snorted in dismissal. "That's dumb. My boys found hardly anything out there *but* papers. The old coot had back-issue newspapers and magazines piled halfway up one wall."

Stringer sipped some more cool refreshment before he explained, "He wouldn't have worried about anyone after him getting their hands on old newspapers. Everyone for miles already knows this town was sort of wild in its day. Steinmuller knew about something more *recent* than the Earp and Clanton feud. As an old newspaper man, he figured that whatever he'd found out would be of interest to the outside world. The one wire we know he sent makes no sense, by itself. I think he began by just posting a letter. He might have thought, at first, it was only what we call a lead, or a tip about odd goings-on that might be worth following up on."

"But you said he sent a wire," Rhodes cut in.

Stringer replied with an annoyed expression, "If you can't pay attention at least let me work it out for myself. The wire services get dozens of letters a day about cake-baking contests and lightning striking a grain elevator. As a small-town newsman he might not have fully grasped that his hot flash from a half-forgotten town would wind up in an unread slush pile. But he should have kept his own copy of it. He should have kept a copy of the much more expensive message he sent by wire when, to him, the story seemed to be breaking in an unexpected way. Most of us in the game make shorthand notes as we go along, too. I didn't find anything out there to indicate he was anything but an old eccentric who like to collect old newspapers."

Wes Rhodes hadn't gotten his job by being a total idiot. He stopped drinking and started smoking, for now, as he mulled this info over a few times. Then he said, with a shrug, "He might have thought he was on to something important. Everyone said he was a mite touched. But, even allowing he'd reported some earlier events afore he sent that wire, it don't make sense no matter how you study on it. Everyone in town already *knew* the mines was flooded. The poor old cuss was just wasting a nickel a word on such a pointless message."

Stringer asked, "If he was just a dotty old hermit, why did someone else feel they needed to kill him?"

"The more I chew this cud the more it looks to me as if we've been trying to play Sherlock Holmes with the disconnections of real life in the real world. That prissy fiddle-playing dope-fiend detective never had to keep law and order in a *real* town on a Saturday night. I'll allow them stories are clever. But they cheat. Old Sherlock never has to work on one alley knifing whilst someone else is beating his old woman to death for unrelated reasons on the far side of the same block."

Stringer protested, "Don't get your bowels in an uproar, Wes. I'm not suggesting we look for mysterious silk threads or even a secret code written with a special ink only one suspect might have hidden behind a secret panel."

But Rhodes insisted, "Yes you are. You keep stringing separate events on one string, as if they all made one pearly necklace. An old man who might have been drunk or dotty sent a meaningless message that was never intended for you in the first place. Then, before you even knew he'd sent it, he got hit by a hunting round as he was wandering about in the hills. It could just as easily been a stray round, fired at a critter a mile or more away. No hunter's about to report firing at a deer or bighorn and *missing* it, is he?"

Stringer said, "That works, to a point. But if that was all

there was to it, how come I had so much trouble getting to Steinmuller's 'dobe in one piece?"

"The troubles and woes you've been having just don't string up with old Dutchy's death," Rhodes said triumphantly, going on to point out, "Let's say your loco notions about the old dead cuss are right. Let's say somebody knew what on earth Dutchy was all hot and bothered about. Let's say they murdered him most foul to shut him up. Then let's say they either found nothing to incriminate them in Dutchy's 'dobe, or, better yet, the old man never had the chance to destroy the evidence and so his killers toted it off with them instead. Then let's both agree all these mighty mysterious events transpired well before you ever started out from Frisco. What motive's left?"

Stringer growled, "Dammit, Wes, if I knew who seemed so anxious to stop me—"

"From doing what?" Rhodes cut in, asking, "From talking to old Dutchy Steinmuller? After he was dead? To keep you from exploring his 'dobe? Why? You did, in the end, and didn't find clue one to pin on anybody! Real life ain't no Sherlock Holmes story, old son. There's a heap of tough and half-cracked folk in this part of the real world. You mixed in a fight in Tucson that you had no damned business mixing in. So it was likely a pal of the late Jesus Garcia that tried to blow you up in bed that time, see?"

Stringer asked, "What about the time Knuckles Ashton tried to kill me in that barber chair?"

"There you go, trying to string all the pearls on the same string again. I've talked to Skagway Sam about that. He says you made Knuckles crawfish, twice, afore he come after you that last time to redeem his rep. Skagway Sam figures his hired-and-fired gun started up with you to begin with because he was the kind of rawhiding asshole Skagway Sam has no use for. I suspect that tinhorn cheats at cards and I know his gal friend is a whore. But I see no reason to doubt his word when he says he figures he owes you a drink more than even one bullet, seeing you saved him a slug in the back that time."

Stringer thought about that as he drained the last of his tame drink, surprised at how soon such fleeting pleasures ended on a really hot afternoon. He decided not to have another as he put the glass back down and said, "You may be right. When they send you to a tough town it's only natural that you might run into tough situations. So, since we both seem to agree I'm just wasting time here, can I go home now, Wes?"

"Old Dutchy ain't in his grave yet," Rhodes answered, shaking his head. "He's barely to Bisbee and a zinc table at the county coroner's. Meanwhile, Knuckles Ashton is out there some fool place with his hide full of holes you punched in the same. I know you ain't guilty of anything serious, Stringer. But until the county says they don't want to discuss such disgusting recent events with you, you'd best stick around."

Stringer swore softly. "Well," he said, "the opera house is closed and Faro Fran objects to my tobacco. Mayhaps I'll just go see if they've got any interesting books at the library."

Wes Rhodes finished his drink and signaled the barkeep for another as he told Stringer, "You'll likely find it closed. I just said you was the least of my worries. The whole infernal town's gone up the slope to watch the scientifical proceedings at the Lucky Cuss. It do sound interesting. But me and my boys have to keep an eye on Allen Street. With even the whores way up the damn mountain, this would be a swell time to rob the bank or crack any number of safes."

Stringer moved closer to the bat wings and stared out soberly at the dead deserted street. He half turned to say, "I thought it was just the heat. But the shadows do seem to be lengthening out there, now. You say everyone's gone up to that abandoned mine?"

Rhodes explained, "It ain't abandoned no more. Some city slickers from L.A. mean to look for more ore down the shaft, if they can ever get it pumped out. That's what they're trying to do right now. Naturally, even the whores are interested. It would be like Tombstone in the old days if it turned out the original mine owners made a mistake." He took a sip from his fresh drink and added, "I frankly think them new boys are full of shit. But, either way, that thumping wonder up the slope is bound to draw trouble like flies when word gets out there even *might* be a new silver rush here."

CHAPTER
EIGHT

Stringer asked directions as the stablehands saddled up old Blue Ribbon for him. But as he rode out he saw he hadn't really needed directions to the thumping wonder and the big crowd it had attracted. He could hear the mighty engine long before he rode into view of the bare slopes of the Dragoon apron and, sure enough, a frothy mixture of mud and evil-smelling water was trying to dig the ditch beside the steep dirt road even deeper as it tore down the slope to wherever water tended to wind up in an otherwise mighty dry land. Stringer was no hydraulic engineer, but he'd covered enough fires to see they were pumping water at a better rate than most fire engines back in Frisco could have managed.

The distance wasn't far. Despite the warmth the low rays of the sun now beat him with, Stringer was almost sorry he'd decided to ride instead of walk. He'd discovered

Blue Ribbon was only halfway trained to respect grounded reins and there wasn't even a solid stump to tether her to as he rode on up to the edge of the crowd and dismounted. As he did so, a pretty gal he'd never seen before in his life grinned at him and asked if he didn't think all this was wonderful. He agreed, to be polite, but in truth all he could see from down here was the backs of heads and a mess of ladies' parasols. He grounded the reins, put a fair-sized stone atop the leather touching dirt, and told Blue Ribbon to behave her fool self.

Then he started to elbow his way farther up the slope, through the whole damned population of Tombstone, it felt like. He worked his way to where a big black hose on the ground was gushing into the ditch. The mine water was coming out cleaner, there, but if anything, more stinky. It reeked of brine and sulfur. He felt sorry for any frogs or pup fish living farther along the wash running into the San Pedro, sooner or later. But Apache and other wild critters had to learn to get along with the white man's manifest destiny if they meant to survive at all.

He found it easier walking atop the big hose along the ditch. As he worked closer to the flat-bottomed bowl cut into the hill around the adit, he finally got his first look at the thumping wonder. The big red engine was mounted on railroad cross ties to dampen its vibrations. It still shook the ground under everyone's feet. Beyond it, yet another big black hose ran into the dark mysterious adit and obviously down the shaft. Some busybody gents in mechanics' overalls tended the big engine or pushed kids back from it, depending on which was causing the most bother at the moment. Over by the adit, in a space kept clear by hard-eyed company police with baseball bats, Stringer

spied Lawyer Lumford and some other important-looking
gents staring into the soggy darkness as if they expected to
see a dragon, or perhaps a princess escaping from one, any
minute. Stringer stayed put and got out his makings as he
studied the scene for himself. He saw the first owners had
salvaged much of the original steam-powered machinery
that should have been up here, along with the tracks that
would have run down the slope where there was now but a
mess of muddy streaks. Some of the old frame and sheet-
iron machine sheds had been left standing, or almost
standing. He saw what appeared to be the stack of a pad-
dle-wheel steamer rising above one rusty rooftop and, seeing the crowd was thinner that way, finished rolling his
smoke, lit it, and ambled over there. Then a mean-looking
cuss with a bat in his hands, a mail-order badge on his
vest, and a Colt .45 on one hip stepped in front of him and
asked, "Where do you think you're going, you silly bastard?"

Stringer smiled thinly back at the hired tough. "I don't
mean to go anywhere on company property that's not allowed. So you win that chip. Now you're going to take
back that part about me being a bastard or I mean to shove
that bat down your throat and bust it off in you."

The hired tough went red-faced and pale-lipped as he
considered Stringer's words. Then, seeing Stringer was
armed, he tossed his bat aside, saying, "You sure talk mean
for such a skinny cuss. But I feel certain you'd like to turn
around and start walking the other way, if you know what's
good for you!"

Stringer shook his head. "I'm waiting for at least a word
of apology. A grudging one will do. I didn't come up here
to find out what was good for me. I understand you have a

job to do and I'll be glad to back off if you'd like to rephrase your request that I do so more politely."

Another, even bigger company man had noticed the tension in the air and drifted over, bat at port arms, to ask quietly if his pard, Rocky, needed any help. Rocky grinned wolfishly at Stringer as he replied, "I don't know. This cowboy says he ain't looking for trouble, but he keeps standing his ground as if he's confused about who's in charge here."

The second one nodded at Stringer. "We're in charge, cowboy. Get back across the ditch with the rest of the rubberneckers, while you can still walk."

Stringer had to think about that. There was less shame in backing down once the odds against one got this serious. But just then Lawyer Lumford came puffing over, demanding, "What's going on here?" Then he recognized Stringer and told his thugs, "It's all right, boys. I'll deal with it."

The two bullies looked disappointed but they must have known who was paying them. They moved off, exchanging confused comments, as Lumford held out a chubby hand to Stringer and said, "It's my fault. I gave orders to keep the crowd back from the machinery and I guess I forgot to say newspapermen were the exception. What would you like to see first, Mr. MacKail?"

Stringer made a mental note that, like most small-town politicos, the fat lawyer was good at recalling names. He shook hands with Lumford and explained, "I'd just like to wander around on my own, if it's all the same to you. I don't have any sensible questions to ask, yet."

Lumford said, "Look about all you like. We've not a thing to hide up here. What we find down at the face, once

we get the shaft pumped out, may be privileged information to be shared only with our stockholders, of course."

Stringer said he understood and that it sounded only
fair. Then he asked, "How long do you figure it's going to
take you and your thumping wonder to drain the mine?"

Lumford shot a fond glance at the big engine across the
way and asked, with a chuckle, "Is that what they've decided to call our big four-banger? It's catchy, next to its
fancy French name. I can't answer your question as to the
time involved. It depends on how much there is to pump."

Stringer raised an eyebrow. "Don't you know?" he
asked.

Lumford shook his head. "Only roughly. When we
bought the quitclaim from the last owners, they told us
they simply had no engineering charts to offer us. They
could give us a rough layout of the main shaft and cross
drifts, of course, but without exact dimensions of a water-
filled chamber we could be talking a lot of gallons, one
way or the other. At the rate the water we can see down the
shaft seems to be receding, however, our own engineers
tell us we ought to pump it dry within twenty-four to sev-
enty-two hours."

Stringer shot a sharp glance across to the big crowd of
local onlookers, but didn't ask the obvious dumb question.
He'd covered enough mildly interesting events to know
that lots of folk seemed ready to just stand there, staring,
by the hour, just in case they *might* get to see something.

Lumford excused himself and headed back to the crowd
of bigshots closer to the adit, lest he forget someone's
name, most likely. It still wasn't clear to Stringer whether
Lumford was just a local lawyer, retained by the silver
speculators to smooth over local matters for them, or

whether he was really as important as he acted.

Stringer was closer to that mysterious smoke funnel than the adit, so he drifted that way, first. The sheet-metal door of the machine shed was ajar on its rusty hinges. He creaked it open to stare into the dark interior, which seemed darker than it really was because of the late-afternoon glare outside. As his eyes adjusted to the gloom Stringer saw the shed was just about filled with the remains of a big Corlis steam pump. It was still in fair shape, thanks to the dry climate. But some belting and of course the gauges and brass valves were missing. He could see why the former owners had abandoned such a whopping mass of iron. In its day, the Corlis had been a thumping wonder of the 1870s. This one, repaired, could no doubt still keep a mine reasonably dry. But despite its size and the fuel it would take to keep it pumping around the clock, no steam engine could lick its weight in internal combustion wang-bangers, no matter what the Stanley brothers said. The railroads and stationary electric plants only clung to steam power because coal was cheaper, where one could *get* it. Aboard a horseless carriage or out here in the middle of nowhere, gasoline power made more sense.

That no doubt accounted for the locked shed built into the hillside beyond the abandoned steam pump. The sign on the door said DANGER HIGH EXPLOSIVES! But it was probably left over from the original mine owners. Those red barrels he'd seen on the wagon back in town had to be stored somewhere up here, even when a curious crowd hadn't gathered to gape and smoke.

Stringer ambled over to the adit. He got a few curious or even annoyed looks from the bigshots assembled there. But the plump Lawyer Lumford said something and nobody yelled at Stringer as he strode to the overhang and peered down the slope into the fetid darkness.

The tramway tracks had been hauled out by the roots to run ore cars somewhere more profitable. The big black intake hose from the thumping wonder ran down the muddy and oil-slicked incline to the greasy surface of the present water level, an impressive ten or twelve yards below the easily read original watermark. Lawyer Lumford and an older gent wearing a peaked cap and a grizzled red beard joined Stringer there. Lumford introduced the older gent as Murdoch Fraser, their consulting engineer. Stringer was too considerate to comment on the fact that Annie had said her uncle had worked in another mine when such skills had been called for in these parts. He had a few harmless secrets he didn't want to discuss with Uncle Murdoch. The old Scot didn't react to Stringer's surname as an Irishman or Italian might have reacted to the name of a fellow countryman. Stringer was used to that. Scots did not automatically greet each other as long-lost brothers in a strange land. They had to think about each other's clans for a while. The history of the Old Country was long, dark, and bloody. It would never do to smile at a man whose great-great-grandfather might have stolen a cow or a wife from one's own ancestors. So the two of them shook, but with a coolness that seemed to confuse the Anglo-Saxon Lumford.

He asked Stringer's opinion of the present waterline. Stringer allowed it was impressive but asked, "How come there's all that grease? It smells like coal oil."

Lumford said, "It probably is. Any lamps left behind when they abandoned the mine would have had some oil in them. Oil floats. The intake is naturally well below that scummy surface, so as we pump the cleaner water out the scum just stays there."

Stringer pointed at the glistening rock and timber props below the original waterline and observed, "No it doesn't. At the rate you're going you're fixing to grease everything up disgusting. If I was running things here, I'd have skimmed all that crud off to begin with and hoped to wind up with a shaft that might dry out clean. Waterlogged rock and timbers tend to stay that way if they're coated with even a thin film of oil."

Murdoch Fraser growled, "Do they, noo? And where might ye have taken a degree as a mining engineer, Mac-Kail?"

Lawyer Lumford seemed an instinctive peacemaker. Before Stringer could respond with answering rudeness, Lumford soothed, "Mister MacKail covered the Alaska gold rush as a newspaper writer, Murdoch. I feel sure he must know something about mining."

"So do I," the old Scot avowed. "Do ye want us to stop and spend a full day skimming yon duck pond so it's fit to swim in or do ye want the damned auld mine pumped oot?"

Lumford shook his jowly head vigorously. "We want to show our stockholders some results before they have to leave. Just carry on and we can always tidy up once we know we have a silver mine and not just a hole in the ground."

With that, he strode away to get out of their line of fire. Stringer gave the older Scot a conciliatory smile. "I'm sorry if I was out of line. I take it you just signed on to pump the shaft out, not to run things once it's dry?"

Old Fraser pursed his lips. "Ay, they offered me the

position of production manager, if and when they need one. But I said I'd take day wages and see that nobody was killed before the daft loons could see for themselves that the Lucky Cuss has seen its day as anything but a mushroom farm. Might MacKail be a sept of a Jacobite clan?"

"It would," Stringer answered, gravely. "We faced the Redcoats at Culloden under the green banner of Lochiel, for all the good it did the cause. Wasn't the high chief of the Frasers drawn and quartered, afterwards?"

The older Scot's eyes grew proud and misty. "Ay, and they still display his false teeth in the Tower of London. From the way they treated *all* of us they captured, we must hae given them a grand scare. Dinna buy any stock in this daft venture, MacKail."

"I never intended to. Are you telling me it's some kind of confidence game?" Stringer prodded.

"I dinna ken what it may be. The only mon in the lot I ken of auld would be Lawyer Lumford. I've ever found him honest, for a mon with an English name. Sae I'd say he was sincerely daft. Whether the others are at larceny or lunacy, there's nae silver left in this mountain. Not high grade enough to pay its way to the surface, anyway. A dollar's worth of silver is best left in the mountain if it takes ye more than a dollar to bring it oot, ye ken."

"I noticed that up Alaska way," Stringer agreed. "There was always some color in the gravel of the gold fields. But only an idiot would pan all day to wind up with less than he could make swamping out saloons."

"Ay, but there's something aboot the very sound of gold or silver that makes many a mon act like an idiot. I've reached an age where I'd rather draw decent day wages than go chasing pipe dreams. They offered me stock in this venture for my services. I said I'd take money if it was all the same to them. Take the advice of a mon wha's chased his share of fairy silver, laddy. Dinna buy in, nae matter what they find at the bottom."

Stringer promised he wouldn't and, having seen about all there was to see until the water level dropped one hell of a lot, he headed back to where he'd left Blue Ribbon.

Pushing through the crowd the other way, he recognized many a face from town. Annie Fraser was standing with another young gal and shot him a warning look before he could howdy her. He did nod at other familiar faces until he bulled out the far side only to see some tents had sprouted like mushrooms on the slope over that way. Through the open fly of one he saw the barkeep from the Oriental Saloon dispensing refreshments over a plank mounted across two barrels. Stringer was only slightly more surprised to spot Faro Fran set up in another tent behind her layout. She was playing solitaire as she waited for the suckers to tire of the action farther upslope. The evening was still young. She looked bored and sort of hazy as well because she was smoking a Havana Perfecto. As she recognized Stringer, standing out in the better light, Faro Fran growled, "The next tent over if you want to get laid, MacKail."

He laughed. "I was wondering where the gals might be. But you do me a disservice, ma'am. I'm too romantic to pay for such pleasures."

She raised her bare shoulders questioningly. "Don't look at me, then, unless you want to try your luck at cards."

He said, "I don't reckon I could afford to play with you either way, no offense. But would you mind telling me how come you got so bothered in that club car the other night, seeing I was only smoking a bitty cigarette?"

The tough redhead removed the big cigar from her painted lips and stared at it as if she'd just noticed it. Then she gave a raucous laugh and clamped it back in place between her teeth as she asked, "Is that the excuse Sam gave for starting up with you?"

"I figured he needed some excuse. But if it wasn't your delicate feelings, what's left?" Stringer inquired.

"Practice, most likely," the brassy dame replied. "Sam has his good points, but he's a natural bully who just can't stand younger and nicer-looking men. Don't get ideas, but that night I did comment that you seemed a nice-looking young gent I might have seen up in Alaska one time."

Stringer said, "I'm sure I'd have remembered, ma'am. You ain't bad-looking, yourself, and if you were there you must have seen how few she-males of *any* variety there were up there. I think I have Skagway Sam figured out. I don't see him about, just now."

She said, "That's because he's keeping an eye on things at the saloon in town. Action or no action, we don't want anyone stealing the whole joint while most of the town seems to be up here. How are they coming with that hole in the ground, by the way?"

"All I saw was a hole in the ground. I wasn't planning on buying any stock in the Lucky Cuss."

"That's too bad," Fran responded wistfully. "I got some I could sell you below face value. That damnfool Sam bought some shares before I could stop him. He won't do that again, if he knows what's good for him."

Stringer smiled thoughtfully. "Oh? I didn't know you was in charge of the outfit, ma'am."

"Sam is the muscle," she replied, "but *I* am the brains.

Lord knows *he* must have been standing behind the privy door when the brains was passed out. He's good at what he does, you understand. It's just that I have to keep telling him he's not supposed to gamble with our money."

"You're the gambler, right?" Stringer said.

"Care for a friendly game of cards, stranger?"

He chuckled at that. "I can see why you were vexed at the notion of a *real* gamble on mining stock. I am inclined to agree with you that only suckers take a chance on losing their own hard-earned money. So I reckon I'll have to pass on your kind offer."

She exhaled more blue smoke, lest fresh air sneak in under the tent fly when she wasn't looking. "You might try one of our other games of chance, then. Go on over to the next tent and tell Mavis I said to give you half-price and your own choice as to what and whom you like best."

"Another time, mayhaps," he said, laughing as he left her to play cards and smoke cigars by herself some more. Passing the bigger tent next door, he spied another lady wearing mostly paint and black lace, sitting listlessly just inside as she filed her nails. Her shape wasn't bad, but it was hard to tell if she was ugly or pretty under all that makeup and an obvious wig. He shot a glance at the nearly setting sun and decided to be true to his librarian, provided he could kill the next few hours without thinking about other temptations.

By the time Stringer had enjoyed a light supper and another dip in the tub down the hall, the sun was setting and it didn't seem as hot, if he left his duds off in the privacy of his room. He knew it was way too early to consider sneaking over to see if Iona-Annie Fraser was still talking to him, so he got out the notes he'd made from old Stein-muller's clippings and tried to get to work on that feature Barca would be expecting.

It wasn't easy. To begin with there were too many names and unimportant charges and countercharges to juggle if one wanted simply to tell the story of the epic battle at—or near—the O.K. Corral. Stringer decided not to include a lot of incidents that, while interesting in their own right, tended to blur the picture and might not have ever really happened.

He wrote his first draft, shorthand, read it over, and decided that while he could doubtless shorten and clarify it well enough once he got back to Frisco, it was just as well he do so now, while he had time to spare and everything fresh in his mind.

It was getting darker in his hotel room. He lit the bed lamp, rubbed his writing hand dry again on the bed linen, and got down to business, writing:

> The notorious feud between the Brothers Earp and the Clanton-McLaurey-Behan faction, which culminated in the so-called gunfight at the O.K. Corral in the autumn of 1881, was less an epic struggle between Good and Evil than the sort of explosion one might hope for by pouring gasoline and nitric acid into the same pickle jar. The tough little town of Tombstone, barely carved out of Apacheria and beset by bewildering political rivalries, simply wasn't big enough to hold such different breeds of self-righteous men at the same time . . .

Quite some time later, Stringer stopped writing and chewed the end of his pencil as he tried to come up with a good ending. There wasn't any. Nobody had won more than a skirmish in a war both sides were fated to lose in the end. For sure, the bloodshed had gone on a spell, with Virgil Earp walking into a shotgun ambush one night as he walked out the Fifth Street entrance of the Oriental, winding up crippled for life and out of the game forever. Morgan would be killed a few months later in that pool hall, leaving only Wyatt Earp, who may or may not have avenged his brothers over at Iron Springs or that night in the Tucson yards, but who'd certainly been run out of the territory, along with Doc Holliday, when the popular and much braver John Slaughter replaced the wishy-washy Behan as county sheriff and proceeded to clean the county up indeed.

Stringer knew Barca would demand more of an ending than what he'd put down on paper so far. But he was just stuck, for now. It hardly mattered that Ike Clanton had come to a bad end in '87 when a federal marshal shot him as a suspected cow thief, or that Old Man Clanton had wound up down in Mexico, raising cows or pushing up daisies, depending on who one might be drinking with at the moment.

Yawning, Stringer heard what sounded like a thunderstorm brewing up outside. He glanced at the window. It was dark enough, now, and when he checked the time he frowned and muttered, "Thunderation indeed! I should have been over to old Annie's an hour ago if I mean to catch her still awake."

That earlier thuderclap he'd heard made little sense to Stringer as he walked along the dark silent street to Annie's place. He could hear the low mutter of the big pump up the slope, once he was outside, but that big bang he'd heard, inside, had been way too loud for the backfire of even a swamping-big gas engine. Thunderstorms, while rare, were not impossible in such dry country. But they usually came with considerable clouds, and the night sky above was so clear it looked as if a man could reach up and scoop stars into his hat if he maybe jumped a mite.

He turned a corner to see the way ahead was a heap more brightly lit. It appeared some fool kids had lit a bonfire in the street up yonder, close to Annie's place. Then Stringer was running as the reality of what he could be looking at sank in.

He'd been right, Stringer saw with a stab of pain, as he bulled on through the thick crowd filling the street between him and the fire. The thick 'dobe walls of the poor gal's house were all that was left, unless one wanted to count roof tiles and busted-up timbers scattered all across her garden and the street out front. As Stringer clung to a tipped gate post, biting his knuckles to keep from screaming out loud, the town law, Wes Rhodes, ambled over to join him, saying, "Evening. You just now get here?"

Stringer gulped and nodded. That answered Rhodes well enough for him to opine, "Looks like your mad bomber struck again. Only this time he flung his dynamite in at a spinster gal who lived all alone. Her name was Iona Fraser. She worked at the library. You wouldn't know her, of course?"

Stringer swallowed a mouthful of bile. "As a matter of fact I did. I'd been by that library more than once. How bad was she hurt?" he asked, already knowing the answer.

Rhodes replied, "Bad enough. We found her head in the alley out back. My boys are still poking about for the other parts that blew through the roof. Them parts still inside won't add up to a bucket of ashes by the time the fire dies down. Some kids was trying to douse the insides with watering cans when we showed up. I told 'em not to. Makes it easier to look for jewelry and such in the trash outside if we have some light on the subject. Can't be nothing inside worth salvaging, now, fire or no fire. That loco bastard used at least six sticks of dynamite, this time."

Stringer asked, white-lipped, "You agree it was the same man, then?"

"Could have just as easily been a woman," Rhodes replied. "Nobody saw nothing, here or over at your hotel. But I'd sure say it was the same maniac at work. How many folk in a town this size could there be with such a peculiar hobby?"

Stringer was about to say something when, across the way, he spotted two deputies hanging on to Murdoch Fraser to keep the distraught old gent from dashing into the burning house. Wes Rhodes said, quietly, "You admitted knowing the gal, MacKail. I'm glad you did, because I'd heard you was spending some time around the library. But a rejected suitor hardly ever tells the law he knew a gal he's just blown up and, if you knew her any better than that, I don't want to hear about it. It ain't right to spread gossip about dead ladies, see?"

Stringer swore under his breath and insisted, "I value her reputation more than you know. But if you think these two attacks with dynamite aren't at all connected, there's something I just have to tell you, Wes!"

Rhodes shook his head and said, "No there ain't. I told you I'd heard gossip about the poor dead gal. To tell you the truth, we was scouting about for an S and W .38 and mayhaps what was left of a roughrider hat, until you showed up just now. Since she was alone in bed when she got blown out of it, that's the way it'll read, officious."

Stringer protested, "I understand your wanting to protect her good name, Wes. But at the cost of covering up for that dynamiter, for God's sake?"

Rhodes shook his head. "Not hardly. When we catch the killer he or she will surely hang high as a Christmas goose. But I'm betting Miss Fraser wasn't the intended target, just now. She was the victim of a dreadful mistake, most likely. Would you care to tell me just where *you've* been, all evening?"

Stringer said, "In my hotel room, writing, since just about sundown. Why?"

Rhodes said, "There you go. If you was alone, writing as silent as me and most folk do, nobody scouting about for you would know where you was. Since they didn't see you anywheres in town they looked, they assumed you might be somewhere you might not want anyone to know about." He pointed his chin at the burning building and added, "They figured a growing boy your age would hardly ever turn in this early, at the hotel, when he had such nice-looking and, some say, willing friends."

Stringer protested, "I've been *trying* to tell you that dynamite was meant for me, dammit."

Wes Rhodes shushed him, cautioning, "Not so loud. I got ears, and a brain as well. I'm taking your word someone's out to kill you. They just misses you some more. If they don't already know you're still alive, they soon enough will, and do they try again, me and the boys figure to catch 'em, see?"

Stringer saw, but asked, "What if they *get* me, the next time they try?"

"If it's any comfort to you, me and the boys will arrest the hell out of 'em, providing we can figure out who done it."

CHAPTER
NINE

Stringer figured Blue Ribbon was safe enough in her stall behind the hotel. But the same couldn't be said for himself or even his notes and other belongings in that room the rascals who were after him knew about. It would have been criminal on his part to stick anyone else with such dangerous quarters, so he paid for another night in the same room at the desk, then asked the night clerk to hire him another, on the same floor, if that could be managed.

The clerk chuckled incredulously. "Surely you jest. I hear one out-of-towner paid a dollar to sleep on the pool table over at the Hatch Joint. As for this here establishment, we got everything but the broom closets booked for the rest of this week. See for yourself."

He spun the open hotel register around to Stringer's point of view on the far side of the counter as he explained, in a joyous tone, "We haven't done business like this since before the mines closed down. Word that they might start up again has drawn the pilgrims from far and wide, see?"

Stringer cast a casual eye on the freshly inked pages and was about to turn away when a bold signature caught his eye and he paused to read it over again. W. R. Hackman was a name to remember indeed if one was in the newspaper game. Stringer had read heaps of Hackman's stuff in the L.A. *Examiner*. Hackman wrote like the old pro he doubtless was and, like Stringer, he specialized in the exposé reporting that could get a reporter in serious fights.

Stringer made a mental note of the room number and just nodded to the clerk while he headed for the stairs as if he'd changed his mind about needing two separate beds for the night. But once he was on the second floor and checking room numbers along the hallway, he saw to his further delight that Hackman's quarters were on the far corner from his and, even better, Hackman's door, if opened just a crack, covered his own empty room's doorway at easy pistol range.

Stringer knocked. There was a short delay, the rustle of cloth on the far side; then a cute little blue-eyed blonde in bare feet and a sky-blue silk kimono opened up to regard him with a mixture of curiosity and distaste. She said, "Yes?" as if she didn't mean it.

Stringer said, "Never mind, ma'am. I thought old W. R. was checked in alone."

But as he ticked his hatbrim to her and started to turn away she said, "I'm W. R. Hackman. What's this all about?"

Stringer had to smile but managed not to laugh as he told her, "I'm Stringer MacKail of the *San Francisco Sun*.

I'd read your stuff and, no offense, I wasn't expecting you to look so ladylike."

"I've read your stuff, too, and I didn't picture you as a saddle tramp," the saucy blonde retorted. "Are you going to come in and tell me what this is all about or am I supposed to catch my death standing here in this drafty doorway? I just took a bath and my hair is wet, dammit."

He said he could see that as he followed her inside her dimly lamplit room. He didn't know her well enough to say how much he liked the smell of a fresh-scrubbed she-male who hadn't spoiled her clean natural odor with perfume yet. She shut the door behind him and leaned her back against it, saying, "If you didn't know I was a woman until just now, is it safe to assume you had something else in mind?"

He grinned down at her. "I was hoping a fellow newspaperman might want to back my play in exchange for sharing a story with me, but——"

"You're on," she cut in flatly, adding, "If you're talking about the venture up at the Lucky Cuss, I fail to see how we could hope to scoop anyone. Aside from at least half a dozen reporters who rode in with me aboard that special train, the local *Epitaph* is still in business and they no doubt have the inside track, here in Tombstone."

Now that he saw how big and tough W. R. Hackman looked, Stringer had no intention of mixing her up in his own problems. But he felt he owed her an explanation and he figured she thought so, too, so he said, "To tell the truth, I don't see how the troubles and woes I've been having could tie into that mine up the slope. Whether they're crooks or not, the new owners have made no secret of their intent to pump out the shaft and sell a mess of mining stock whether there's anything there or not. They seem to want all the publicity they can get and, to date, few if any other reporters have been called upon to duck. I seem to be the only newspaper cuss for miles that's in trouble. If I knew why, I'd know who was behind it."

He gave her a quick recap of his recent adventures, leaving out the parts involving poor Annie and the mysterious Miss Tillie in Tucson. When he'd brought her up to date the petite blonde said, soberly, "They think you know something, or someone, and they don't want some secret printed in the *Sun* or any other papers. I read some of the stories you filed from Alaska a few years back. I thought your well-worded warning about salted mines was past due. How do you like the idea that someone's trying to keep you from exposing another such flimflam, here in Tombstone?"

He shook his head. "That occurred to me before I knew they were selling stock and running special trains in here for potential investors. Any decent reporter would consider such salting and, like I just said, none of the rest of you have drawn half as much fire as me."

She insisted, "But you're more expert than the rest of us on the subject, having already exposed such dirty doings up in Alaska more than once. I admired your piece on the crooked rodeo judges up in Cheyenne that time, too. There were other reporters in the stands then, but you were the only one with enough cowboy in your walk to spot angles the more citified boys failed to see, staring right at 'em, correct?"

He replied modestly, "It wasn't my fault I was raised more rustic and might have known a mite more about riding and roping. I'm not a mining engineer and, even if I was, I'd have a time salting a mine in full view of the reporters and at least some canny investors who'll surely be there once the Lucky Cuss has been pumped dry."

She asked, "What if they salted it in advance, before it was flooded?"

"How? The mine was in the hands of honest owners who'd have never allowed it to fill with ground water if they'd thought there was any silver ore left. Even if they hadn't been all that honest and let's say been out to unload a worthless mine on other suckers, they'd have done so then and there. They'd have never waited till the shaft was too full of water to show the suckers anything. In the end, they sold the property, as almost worthless property, to the present owners. Said syndicate seems to be going to considerable expense to pump the mess out and see what's at the bottom. Whether they're sincere mining men or not, I don't see how they could have salted the bowels of the earth under hundreds of feet of water. A man in a diving suit can't work that deep and, if a diver could, I can't see how any of the usual salting tricks would work underwater."

"They usually load a big shotgun with grains of precious metal instead of lead and just blast away at the rock, right?" the blonde asked.

"That only works for gold," Stringer corrected her. "Anyone who accepted grains of chopped-up silverware as a silver strike would have to be sort of dumb about silver mining. Gold and some native copper shows up as specks of pure metal in the rock. But silver ore is almost always a chloride or sulphide that looks more like inky salt. You have to know what you're doing if and when you're prospecting for silver or, for that matter, trying to salt a vein with it. They use a big vet's hypodermic—it has to be a glass one—to inject silver mixed with acid into the cracks. The acid reacts with the natural rock and the final results are thin veins of silver salts."

"Even I can follow that," she said, tossing her damp blond locks. "What if, just as the mine was shutting down, some slicker with an eye to the future sneaked down to the face with a horse-doctor's needle and—"

"It won't work," Stringer cut in, explaining, "Even if someone thought that far ahead, he couldn't have driven the acid all that deep into the rock and by now that water, under considerable pressure near the bottom, would have leached his handiwork out of the cracks. Water under pressure is a pretty good solvent on its own. That's how a lot of ore veins get under a mountain to begin with. The crooks after me have to be worried about some *other* business they've been up to."

She didn't look too convinced, but she said, "All right. There must be a lot of crooked ways to get rich in a town that's just starting to come back to life. How are we going to set about catching them?"

"We are not going to do anything" he told her with a sigh. "Before I found out you were a gal I had a half-baked plan to have a fellow male spell me off and on at a door crack in hopes they might try again at my room down the hall, but—"

"I have a gun," she cut in, adding, "A girl traveling alone just never knows when she might need one. It's a Harrington and Richardson .32 revolver. I wasn't sleepy, anyhow. If we took turns on watch the single bed I booked over there ought to be enough for the both of us."

He shot a wistful glance at the narrow brass bedstead

against the far wall and said, "Thanks, but no thanks. A man who'd hide behind a woman's kimono would eat stuff I'd rather not mention in front of a lady."

She flared her nostrils at him, demanding, "Are you one of those he-brutes who consider us the frailer sex?"

He was forced to reply, honestly, "Whether I'm a brute or not, you *are* a heap more petite than me or your average hired gun, ma'am. I didn't plan it that way any more than you did. I've never read where the Lord asked Adam's advice on the use of that rib Adam lost under general anesthetic, either. So go fuss at the Lord or, if you'd just as soon have it Professor Darwin's way, go fuss at Mother Nature. Us poor men never asked to be stuck with the chore of shifting heavy furniture, you know."

She said, "Pooh, I could lick both my brothers and I'm pretty good with a gun, too."

"I'll take your word on that," he said. "You write hard-boiled enough for any man, too. But at the risk of insulting you I still don't want you mixed up in any gunplay. So I'd best skin the cat some other way."

"Damm it," she protested, "you said you'd share a scoop with me if I helped you!"

"I know I did. I will, providing you let me handle things my own pigheaded he-male way." When she agreed that sounded fair, he continued, "I'd like to leave my possibles and some notes I made in here with you. Then I mean to find safer quarters for the night. Don't ask me where. If you don't know, you can't say, no matter who asks. When I leave I want you to bolt your door behind me and stay put till I get back here after sunrise. Do just as I say and I'll be proud to take you up to the Lucky Cuss with me as soon as they get her pumped out."

"I'm holding you to that, MacKail. But what if you don't come back?"

"Start without me," he suggested. "If the rascals seemed likely to know where I mean to fort up for the night, I wouldn't be heading that way. But you never know. So far, the sneaky cusses have been outsmarting me pretty good. If you wind up writing my obit try to remember I spell it S-T-U-A-R-T, not S-T-E-W-A-R-T. I just hate Stew, don't you?"

Even though the moon shone bright the Turkey Creek wagon trace was sort of graveyard gloomy after dark. The fact that they'd found Johnny Ringo dead around here, propped up against the base of a tree with a bullet in his brain and a six-gun in his lifeless hand, didn't help to cheer things up; nor did an owl, who may have known something Stringer didn't know, hooting a mournsome howdy as he passed. Some said poor Ringo had been bushwacked up this way by Buckskin Frank Leslie, while others were as sure the morose gunslick had taken his own life. Either way, old Ringo was said to ride this very trail at night aboard a pallid ghost pony that glowed in the dark just like Ringo did.

Stringer hoped gents in the habit of throwing dynamite were more afraid of ghosts than he was. Since he'd ridden out of town discreet, and anyone who wanted to scout old Dutch Steinmuller's place had already done so, he hoped, there'd be no sensible reason for anyone to think of searching there again for anything or anybody. Stringer wasn't about to bed down on a dead man's bunk, but if he stretched out on those bales of newsprint and covered up with his rain slicker, he ought to be able to catch forty winks safely enough.

Knowing the way helped him get there quicker this time. But as he rounded the last bend he spied light through a window of the old man's 'dobe and reined in, muttering, "Shit."

Then he rode back and off the trail a piece to tether Blue Ribbon in a copse of mesquite so he could move in afoot, sidearm already drawn. As he eased closer he could make out two ponies tethered in front. That put their riders inside and not on guard. They'd have had the ponies safer in the back corral if they were worried about unexpected visitors. They read as a pair of cowhands riding in who'd stopped to explore the empty 'dobe. By now the neighborhood kids no doubt had old Dutchy Steinmuller acting as a local haunt as well.

Nevertheless, Stringer kept his gun out and his booted feet as quiet as he could until he was just outside the open side window. He was glad he had when he heard a slap, followed by a she-male sob of pain. Then a man's voice growled, "You can do better than that, señorita. Tell me what you was truly after, here, afore I really hit you good!"

A girl's voice, flavored with chili pepper, protested, "In the name of Jesus, Maria, *y* Jose, I have told you all I know! My own poor *papacito* was a friend of the poor *viejo* who used to live in this *casita*. I was only searching for mementos of my family that might have been left here."

Stringer cautiously moved close enough to see inside. He saw the Mex gal was younger and prettier than he pictured her. The Anglo gent standing over her as she sat bound to an old chair was even uglier than expected.

Stringer didn't need the sketch Homer Davenport had drawn for him to decide the cuss was the same one who'd been glaring at his back aboard that coast train. The bushy-browed brute was glaring pretty good at his she-male victim as he growled, "Let's see if I got this straight. You claim you're the granddaughter of old Pedro Morales, the charcoal burner who died a few weeks ago, up in these hills. You say you was only on your way to his charcoal camp to salvage rosary beads and such he might have been buried with when you spied this place by the light of the moon and decided you might as well rob it too, right?"

She shook her head frantically, protesting, "I am no thief! You can see for yourself there is nothing of value here. I only wished for to, how you say, look around?"

The husky bastard, who'd obviously caught her at whatever she'd been doing, cast a weary eye about the dusty interior of the tiny 'dobe and decided, "Well, you could be telling me true. You ain't the first who's prospected this abandoned claim, you know, and if there was one thin dime to be found out here, me and the boys would have found it."

Then he drew his .45 and, as her sloe eyes widened in pure horror, he told her, amiably enough, "It's too bad you're such a nosy little thing. You're sort of pretty. But I'm not supposed to be in these parts, official . . . so it's been nice talking to you."

Stringer and the girl both had to assume he meant it when he began to cock the single-action hammer. It was considered pure murder to gun a man without calling him, and pure suicide to do so when his gun was out and cocked, so Stringer aimed at the son of a bitch's gun hand as he fired first.

His risky showboat shot worked. The beetle-browed gunslick's pistol flew one way as it went off harmlessly and he flew another, howling like a gut-shot coyote as he hit the front door and just kept going in a cloud of splinters while Stringer yelled after him to stay put and explain his unseemly manners.

The cuss didn't even stop for his pony. As Stringer heard him crashing across the stony creekbed and up the far slope through the moonlit chaparral he decided that since first things should come first, chasing a wounded grizzly through bushes might not be it. He tore around to the gaping doorway, ran inside, and doused the lamp as the startled Mex gal gasped, "Oh, you just saved my life, señor!"

He said, "Not yet," as he moved over to her, holstered his .38, and got out his pocket knife to cut her free. Then he hauled her out front, put her aboard one of the ponies, mounted the other, and hung on to her reins to lead her back to where he'd left Blue Ribbon. As he helped her down he said, "Now I've saved your life. Which one of these ponies was yours to begin with, Miss . . . ah . . . ?"

"Concepción Morales," she replied, adding, "My pony is the pinto you were just riding. I would have told you, *pero—*"

"Never mind," he snapped, "Get on him, now, and hold my old Blue Ribbon steady whilst I see if there's any calling cards in that rascal's saddlebags. You could save us some time if you could say you already knew him, *querida.*"

"I never saw him before," she explained tossing her head in the moonlight. "He came in on me as I was rummaging through those old newspapers, just a few moments ago."

Stringer swore softly. "It's tough to search saddlebags for clues when there ain't no saddle bags. This looks like a livery nag. We'll just let him go, and it might be more interesting, come morning, to see just where it goes home to and what they recall about bushy eyebrows. Now we'd best get you out of here before he comes back for his horse, with pals."

As he mounted beside her, Concepción dimpled at him and said, "I am sure we saw the last of that one. Where did you learn to shoot like that?"

He said, "I'd rather hear where you live. We can tell stories after I get you home safe."

She nodded and took the lead, straight uphill, saying, *"Bueno.* I was on my way to my grandfather's when that *lobo* must have taken me for *Capotita Colorada,* no? Is not far. Only steep in a few places."

He chuckled and told Little Red Riding Hood, in his lingo, to lead on. But after she'd done so a spell, it commenced to get steep indeed. He called out, "For Pete's sake, neither of us are riding mountain goats. What did you say your late grandfather was, an eagle?"

She assured him cow ponies could make it, adding, "Before he was found dead, down below on the trail beside his burro, my poor grandfather gathered and prepared charcoal for to sell in Tombstone. His last camp, of course, had to be far enough from town for to find any *robles* left. Oh, forgive me, you call them *oaks,* no?"

He started to tell her he spoke Spanish, but decided not to, just yet. He still didn't know who else they might be meeting up with, and it was surprising what some would say in front of a dumb gringo at times. They topped the crest and she led him on down the back slope. He didn't ask why. He knew mesquite made better firewood as it was, and nothing else seemed to be growing around here. They crossed another dry creekbed and bulled up yet another steep slope, with the chaparral getting thicker, now. As they approached the next crest and Stringer spied a lightning-blasted oak outlined against the sky beyond, she turned in her saddle to announce, "We are almost there."

He said, "In that case, you'd best ride in well ahead and explain my honorable intentions. No offense, Concepción, but this won't be the first time I've escorted a Spanish-speaking lady home."

She laughed. "My brothers are all down in Bisbee with our parents, tonight. The family moved down there when things got so slow in Tombstone. *Pero* our stubborn grandfather said he liked it better up here in the Dragoons and you know how some old men are, no?"

He replied, "Some old women, too, when you study on old-timers. But what was your grandfather living on, up here on his own? He couldn't have sold much charcoal once the mines shut down, could he?"

She shook her head. "They say in Tombstone's days of glory our whole family could not have provided enough charcoal for to run the mine pumps. They just burned mesquite, even green, and let the smoke blow about as it would. My grandfather sold clean-burning charcoal only to the housewives in town, for to cook and heat with. Oak charcoal burns with no smoke at all if one knows how to use it. Is true most of his Anglo customers moved away when the mines and a lot of other businesses shut down. *Pero* was still enough tidy Anglo women to buy all the charcoal one old man and his burro could deliver. That is for why I wish to search about his camp. He had little *dinero* in his pockets when they found him dead. He was a simple man with no need for expensive pleasures. We found it *curioso* that nobody up this way could tell us where the rewards of all his hard labor might be."

By this time they'd topped the rise. Stringer saw the sort of giant beaver lodge the old man had been burning charcoal in when he'd still been able to get around up here. There was a smaller but still impressive woodpile as well. The moonlight gleamed on an ax imbedded in a partly split oak log. Beyond the working parts of the camp stood a canvas tent, still taut despite the winds that must have blown across this ridge, since the old man had staked it securely, like the old hand at camping out he must have been. Concepción dismounted first to rummage inside the tent while Stringer tethered their two ponies to a pair of oak stumps as she'd apparently expected him to. Unlike that bossy little blonde from the *Examiner,* this gal didn't seem to mind being a poor frail she-male.

As he strode over to the tent fly, Stringer called into the dark interior for any oats she might have noticed in there. She backed into view, hauling a dusty burlap sack she felt might be full of cracked corn, at least. When Stringer opened it, it was. He gazed about until he spotted an old cooking pot and packed it back to the ponies as well. He watered both from his canteen. Then he left each a pile of cracked corn to work on, telling them, "I know you'd like to go to bed with more supper. I would, too. But that's life."

As he rejoined Concepción by the tent he saw she'd spread some bedding on the sand out front, albeit still under the fly. She said, "I have some tortillas *y* frijoles as well as some pulque in my saddlebags. Why do you not build a fire as I make ready for to cook, eh?"

He shook his head. "Lighting a night fire in Apache country can get you in trouble even when there are no Apache for miles. I ate a real supper earlier. You should have, too, if you ain't on a diet. Dry tortillas washed down with pulque sounds okay to me."

She didn't argue. Soon they were reclining side by side under the tent fly, enjoying, or trying to enjoy, pasteboard-flavored tortillas and warm pulque. Both were acquired tastes. Pulque was fermented maguey juice, partway to becoming tequila, which tasted more like liquor and less like soap. But though not yet distilled to hard liquor, pulque could do the job on you if you mistook it for a home brew mild as beer or even wine. So despite the healthy thirst one got from chewing dry tortillas—like blotting paper—Stringer tried to take it easy as they passed the clay jug back and forth.

Little Concepción was less inhibited, if not thirstier. She was full of plans for a treasure hunt, come sunrise. It sounded tedious to him. On the other hand, it wasn't his money they were talking about. He said, "I'll help you scout about as soon as it's light enough. But unless your grandfather hid a can of coins pretty obvious, you'd best streak for home and come back with some armed relations, Concepción. Aside from the sheer toil involved in scalping this whole mountain, that ruffian who was about to kill you when I showed up might want to go a second round with you."

She snuggled closer atop the bedding to say, "Pooh,

nobody else knows where this camp is. It is cold up here at night without a fire, no?"

"You'd best get under the blankets, then. I'll keep an eye open, just in case you're wrong."

She didn't have to be asked twice. He knew she was used to living in close quarters, where personal privacy took more than a little ingenuity. So he was surprised if not exactly upset when she proceeded to shuck her duds before she crawled under the blankets instead of waiting till after. He assumed she felt it was dark enough to get away with that. It wasn't. She sure was a hairy little thing. Her nipples matched her sloe eyes as well, by moonlight. Then he got to observe her shapely naked rump for a spell as she took her own good time crawling into the bedding. He looked away and reached absently for his Bull Durham pouch, but she demanded, "For why are you still sitting there with all your clothing on? Do you not wish to come to bed with me?"

He turned his head to see her sloe eyes smoldering up at him and had no trouble at all recalling the other parts of her the bedding was covering now. He said, "I'm not sure that huntsman who saved Little Red Riding Hood got to molest her, afterwards. You're just a kid, Concepción. You don't know how inevitable things can get, once the purest-minded gent's under the covers with a gal in your present state of undress."

She pouted up at him. "Ay caramba! Have you no feelings for a *muchacha* in distress?"

He laughed and told her he was starting to feel distressed, too, adding, "It's one thing to be a mite drunk on moonlight and pulque. It can be another thing entire to wake up in the cold gray dawn with a headache and second thoughts."

"Pulque never gives me a headache," she sniffed. "Do you scorn me because I am not one of your blue-eyed Anglo *muchachas?*"

That did it. Having had to pass on a half-dressed blue-eyed blond *muchacha* that same evening, it was asking too much of any natural man to expect him to pass on a stark-naked and apparently willing brunette. So he assured her that scorning her was the furthest thing from his mind and proceeded to get out of his own duds and into the bedding with her.

But when he took her shapely nude body in his arms and hauled her close to kiss her, Concepción stiffened and gasped, "What is this I feel between us, down here?"

Considering she had her hand around it at the moment, Stringer thought that a mighty dumb question. He held her less tightly and asked, "What were you expecting, flowers?"

She giggled and clasped his erection tighter as she replied, "I was not expecting so much of anything! Anglo women must be built like cows!"

He nibbled her ear and rolled her on her back as he assured her, "Of course, if you'd rather not . . ."

She put both arms around him to welcome him aboard. Then they both gasped in mingled pleasure and concern as he entered her with difficulty. After that, of course, they were free to go lovingly loco for a while, and did.

Later, as they shared a smoke and more cuddles, Concepción marveled in an adoring tone, "That was *muy romantico, querido*. I am so glad I did not know what was getting into me until we got it in me. I fear I would have resisted your advances if I had known how big you were, in every way. *Pero* now that you have made me so brave about such matters, could we do it again before we go to sleep?"

He took a drag on their smoke and assured her it wasn't all that late, yet. She snuggled closer and repressed a yawn to ask, *"Es verdad?* I am more used to going to bed with the chickens. For why do you stay up late? What is there to do at night, out of bed, I mean?"

He patted her bare bottom with his free hand as he told her, chuckling, "Nothing's better than this, night or day. But if I was alone with a lamp, right now, I'd probably be working on my notes. I told you I was a newspaperman on our way up here, remember?"

She said, "Sí, like Señor Steinmuller, my grandfather's poor amigo. Do you know for why they both died within the very same month, *querido?* I find this most unusual, no?"

He took another drag and snuffed out the butt in the sand beside him as he said, "That's one of the news angles I'm still working on. I know how Steinmuller died; he was shot. I don't know exactly what killed your grandfather a few days earlier. An old man could die just as easily from a natural cause or a less natural blow on the head. Steinmuller might have been wondering about that, too. He was snooping around out in the high chaparral when somebody put that rifle round in him and he barely made it home to die."

She began to toy with the hairs on his belly as she mused, half to herself, "I wonder what that wicked gringo you saved me from thought to find in the poor dead *viejo's* 'dobe. From the way he behaved, at first, I think he thought I knew what it might be."

Stringer shrugged the bare shoulder her head wasn't resting on. "I scouted about for a sign, back there, right after I found him there. The town lawmen who drove out to pick up the body no doubt poked about as well. But you may have something, Concepción. That bushy-browed bully boy wouldn't have been there at all tonight if his side wasn't still hunting for something they suspect old Steinmuller had on him the day he died."

She began to walk her fingers down his belly, teasingly, as she sighed and said, "I found nothing of value. Even the postage stamps had been canceled."

He yawned. "I noticed. You mean those few envelopes in the trunk at the foot of his bed, right?"

She answered, *"Pero* no, I meant the stamps on all those old letters I found under those old newspapers."

Stringer perked up to demand, *"Under* those old back issues over against that one wall? You looked?"

She said, "Sí. Under one end of the pile, near the wall. I could see no treasure had been buried where the dirt floor was bare. So I shifted the pile, just a little, for to see if perhaps the dirt looked softer there. When I saw all those gringo stamps I thought they might be worth something. Alas, they had all been canceled. As I was going through the envelopes, for to see if there was any *dinero* in any of them, I heard that wicked hombre coming. So I simply shoved the newspapers back against the wall the way I found them. The rest you know."

He propped himself up on his elbow, muttering, "Not by half. I have to get back there as soon as it's light enough to see what I might be doing. Meanwhile, you say you opened some of those envelopes, *querida?*"

She said, "No. I opened all of them. Most were empty. One had been stuffed with slips of colored paper—*verde, amarillo, rosado*—and some just *blanco*. I think he may have put them all together in one envelope. Aias, I do not read much *inglés. Pero,* wait, I think some were from a Señor *Hearst*. Would that mean anything to you?"

He bent over to kiss her before he said, "You bet your sweet bottom it might! It sounds as if the old man was collecting a heap of rejection slips!"

"Are these good for to collect? They only seemed bits of paper to me," she replied.

Stringer explained, in simple terms she'd be able to grasp, how little any writer enjoyed the sight of a rejection slip paper clipped to a story sent back to him. He added, half to himself, "If the old man just kept sending his whatever out again, it's in some editor's slush pile tonight instead of his 'dobe. There's no sense looking for it there and Lord knows when they'll get around to either running it or sending it back. So, let's see, the old man sent some news item over and over again to no avail. It must have struck everyone as mighty uninteresting if the Hearst Syndicate turned it down. They just love stories about two-headed calves and spooks."

She sighed. "I wish you would make up your mind if you wish for to make love again or talk about two-headed calves. If the old newspaperman had written something interesting, someone would have wanted it, no?"

Stringer said, "Hold the thought about whose turn it might be to get on top, for now. The beads are starting to string together. Let's say the old man filed a story that read sort of so-what. Let's say he kept submitting it, with no luck, until something even more exciting happened and he sent that wire, all het up right before someone gunned him to keep him from doing just that."

She asked, hopefully, "Do you think he knew who killed my grandfather, or where my grandfather hid his *dinero?*"

Stringer thought before he muttered, "Steinmuller wasn't out to report a murder. He only wired that the Tombstone Lode was still flooded, which was hardly news. The wire service wouldn't have picked up on it at all if they hadn't made the mistake of assuming it was the town, not the old mines above it, that suffered said flood. So what could I be missing, dammit?"

She suggested, "Maybe he was only loco. For why else would he hide worthless paper under other worthless paper? Oh, that gives me another idea. What if my grandfather hid his *dinero* under that big woodpile, *querido?*"

Absently, he said, "I'll help you look for it at sunrise. Then, either way, I have to get back to town. There's something about that last wire the old man sent that I have to be missing. Lord knows it was short enough. At a nickel a word he couldn't afford to be long-winded and . . . That's it! He blocked out his message free-style and then, to save money, he crossed out all the words he thought he could get away with. Only he crossed out one word too many. Put back just one word and the whole thing makes sense at last!"

Concepción replied in a languorous tone, *"Bueno.* Can we make love some more, now?"

CHAPTER
TEN

Between having Concepción for breakfast, helping her find her grandfather's tin box of silver dollars under the woodpile where she'd correctly guessed it might be, and then searching the old 'dóbe some more after sending Concepción on her way in a very good mood indeed, Stringer didn't get back to Tombstone until fairly late in the morning.

He still had some loose strings to tie up. It wasn't easy with most of the town up at the Lucky Cuss. The shaft was said to be just about dry by now and nobody wanted to miss the first assay on the first rock they brought up. But he found an old printer sticking type in the press room of the *Epitaph* and, since the local newspaperman was a real pro who could read copy and carry on a conversation at the same time, Stringer was able to confirm a few notions he'd been mulling over all morning. He dropped by the marshal's office and swapped notions with Wes Rhodes long enough to burn a smoke down. All he came away from there with, for sure, was that nobody had shown up in town, official, with bushy brows and a gunshot wound and that Knuckles Ashton was alive and well, or at least alive, in the El Paso jail. The butt-shot Knuckles had gone to an El Paso M.D. for treatment, the doc had told the law about it, and the Texas Rangers had recalled they had an outstanding warrant on the rascal.

Nobody but one sleepy barkeep could be found at the Oriental Saloon. He told Stringer that Faro Fran and the gals were all up to the Lucky Cuss either to console the losers or help the winners celebrate. Some gents always called for wine and women, either way Dame Fortune dictated. Stringer thanked him for the information and tried farther along Allen Street, deserted as if it was midnight rather than just about noon.

As he'd hoped he might, Stringer caught up with Skagway Sam at the same pool hall, enjoying a solitary game of eight ball. The burly tinhorn was playing in his vest and shirtsleeves. The place was otherwise empty. As Stringer entered, Skagway Sam told him, "Go into the tap room next door and help yourself to some cold cuts and beer, if you know how to work the tap. Everyone's gone up to that infernal mine to stand about and stare at nothing in the hot sun. I has it on good authority that they won't be blasting this side of three, Lord willing and the creeks don't rise."

Stringer hung up his hat but said, "I washed some pigs' feet down with lager the moment I got back to town, say an hour or so ago. Tortillas and pulque's just not my notion of proper breakfast."

"Mine, neither," said Skagway Sam, pointing his own

cue at the wall rack as he asked, "Care for a game, old son?"

"I'll just watch, for now. I had a rough night and my head's just starting to clear."

Skagway Sam shrugged, told Stringer to suit himself, and bet, "Six ball in the corner pocket," which he proceeded to sink with almost disinterested grace. Then he said, "Ten ball in the side pocket. Were you aiming to put me in your paper as the all-time pool shark of Tombstone, Stringer?"

In the dimly lit room Stringer began to roll himself a smoke, leaning back against one wall, as he replied, "Not as an all-time pool shark. I'd have thought high rollers like you and Miss Faro Fran would have aimed higher than Tombstone when you came back down from the Alaska gold fields. No offense, but this town was about dead when you first got here."

Skagway Sam paused to chalk his cue tip as he met Stringer's eyes with a casual smile and said, "Dead's a strong word. They like to say, here, that Tombstone is too tough to die. I will allow we've been hoping someone would wake it up a mite more, though. What do you figure they'll find, up the slope, when they bust some fresh rock off the old face?"

Stringer said, flatly, "Silver. Mayhaps a mite low grade, but I'm sure it'll assay rich enough to encourage deeper digging, with another stock issue to pay for it, of course. Old Ferris, over to the *Epitaph,* assured me the ore samples will be assayed by a reputable old-timer everyone here in town has always found dead-on-the-level honest, too."

Skagway Sam sighed wistfully. "Damn! I wanted in on the Lucky Cuss. I even bought some shares in it a while back. But old Fran called me a damn fool and made me get rid of 'em at face value. Four ball in the far corner pocket."

Stringer waited until the gambler had sunk the shot before he struck a match to light his smoke, then said, "That was smart of her. She no doubt wanted it distinctly understood that neither of you had any interest at all in silver mining, once the fur starts to fly. They don't know they know it at the *Epitaph*, yet, but once the sheep figure out they've been shorn, it's just bound to occur to everyone that while the syndicate promoting that grand reopening was Los Angeles based, they made a point of hiring a lot of local Tombstone help."

Skagway Sam called a shot and missed. He straightened up to reach for the chalk cube again as he muttered, "Tip slipped on that last one. What was that about shearing sheep, just now?"

Stringer blew a smoke ring to study as he explained, "Oh, the whole thing's a con job. The Lucky Cuss has been salted. Didn't you know that?"

Skagways Sam growled, "Not hardly. Old Fran said it could all be a flimflam when she made me unload that stock. Others here in town have opined they couldn't see why the original owners had pulled up stakes and just about given the claims away, after a good twenty years of mining, if there was anything left to mine. On the other hand, all the mining men I've jawed with on the subject agree there's just no way to salt a mine when it's under tons and more tons of deep dark water."

"They were right," Stringer agreed. "It couldn't be done that way. So they had to do it another way. They began by buying the claim as it was, a worthless water-filled hole in the ground, cheap. Then they posted it against trespassing and put guards up there as well to make sure nobody strayed too close to the adit."

Skagway Sam grimaced as he bent over the table again, saying, "Sure they did. Then they sent someone down the shaft in a diving suit to hammer silverware into the considerably flooded face, right?"

"Stringer countered." "They didn't have to, first they simply repaired the old steam pump. It only took, say, one barrel of spare parts that screwed off again just as easy. Once they had the old pump working again, silent as any other stationary steam engine, they filled the firebox with smokeless charcoal they bought off an old Mexican recluse, and started her up. They only pumped at night or mayhaps when it was raining, of course. Somebody might have noticed running water, other times."

Skagway Sam frowned hard at the cue ball, then growled, "Nine ball, side pocket. I can see how your notion might work, if someone was drunk, crazy, or both. Why on earth would they have hauled that big thumping gasoline engine up the mountain if they already had the old steam pump working?"

Stringer chuckled. "That's easy. They hope to prove their sincerity and no doubt amuse a bigger crowd with that huge red thumping wonder, while, naturally, few of us were supposed to even think about the old steam pump that had kept the shaft dry a good twenty years. If anyone looked, as I did, they could see it was busted and, hell, if it was any *good,* as you just pointed out, the thumping wonder would have been a needless expense."

He took another drag before he continued, "Getting back to before they'd sold enough stock to buy such amusing toys, the promoters pumped the shaft dry, the old-fashioned way, and they they simply went down to the face and salted it in any number of the usual methods. We'll know more about that once they pass out some ore samples, any minute, now. Once they had the mine salted they smeared plenty of grease over the face to waterproof it. Then they poured some more oil about to make sure the whole shaft would seem as disgusting after the water level rose and sank in one more cycle. After that, they just had to wait a few days and, sure enough, the springs of ground water that had called for hard pumping in the first place filled the shaft back up and they were ready to raise the curtain on the final act, which is going on right about now, with a whole trainload of potential investors and dumber reporters than me on hand to watch them hit silver some more."

Stringer dropped his burned-down smoke to the floor and ground it out with a bootheel as the pool room suddenly commenced to look more crowded. One of the three foppishly dressed but seriously armed newcomers stared soberly at Stringer as he asked Skagway Sam, "Are you having any trouble with this cowboy, boss? Miss Fran said you might."

Skagway Sam straightened up, lay his cue on the green felt, and smiled knowingly at Stringer as he almost purred, "I ain't sure, yet. The more he keeps jawing the more I suspicion he could be out to put me ahint the eight ball. Is that what you was getting at, old son?"

Stringer smiled back. "Gee," he said, "I thought Miss Faro Fran was up at the mine. I can see why she might not want to be on record as an interested spectator, though. You know, Sam, if you put on your own frock coat the four of you would look a lot like the Earps and Doc Holliday

must have looked to poor young Billy Clanton that time.
He was dressed more cow, like me."

Skagway Sam didn't seem to find this at all amusing.
He said, "You was leading up to something afore you noticed my boys, here. You'd have gone to the law with it if
you was only out to accuse them L.A. city slickers and
nobody else, right?"

"Yep. Shall I go on with my story, gents?" Stringer
asked, scanning the room.

Skagway Sam growled, "You'd better. I'd like to hear
just how much you really know."

Stringer frowned thoughtfully. "Let's see, where were
we? Oh, right, they didn't want the old Mex charcoal
burner to gossip about all the smokeless fuel he'd sold before they'd bought the fancy new gas pump, so he died on
the Turkey Creek wagon trace one morning. It wouldn't
have taken much skill, or courage, to kill one old unarmed
man. But they must have done him in too late. He had an
old pal, Dutchy Steinmuller, and they no doubt exchanged
comments on the weather and anything else they found
interesting, every time the one old man passed the other
old man's 'dobe. The old Mex would have been a simple
soul. Dutchy Steinmuller was an old newspaperman who
still had a nose for news.

"Once he found out his old pal was selling one hell of a
heap of charcoal at the Lucky Cuss, Steinmuller surely
snooped a mite. He found out they'd pumped the shaft dry,
not long before his old pal died so mysterious. So he reported it to the outside world the only way he knew how.
Not knowing whether he could trust the one paper in town,
he sent his story to all the big news syndicates. They didn't
find his story nearly half as interesting as he did. Why

should any editor in, say, Chicago or even L.A. find it interesting that someone was pumping out an old mine? That's what mine pumps are made for, right?"

"I wouldn't know. I've never worked in no damn mine," Skagway Sam remarked in distaste.

Stringer agreed grimly, "That's for certain. Tinhorns like you and your late pard, Soapy Smith, go in for less sweaty ways to get rich quick. The out-of-town promoters had no trouble hiring men to do the hard work. Some of 'em, like Lawyer Lumford and old Murdoch Fraser, were just honest dupes. They'd have wanted as few known crooks as possible connected with their enterprise. That's why the brains of your own particular outfit, Miss Faro Fran, got so upset when she caught you getting close enough to the mine-stock promoters to cadge some stock off them. She wanted it cash and carry with no connections on paper between you and them. She'd made a deal with them to handle rough stuff that didn't tie in too close with the Lucky Cuss, right?"

Skagway Sam's voice was tabby-cat gentle as he asked, "What rough stuff might we be talking about, old son?"

Stringer shot a knowing albeit somewhat worried smile at the four armed men who had him boxed against the rear wall of the pool hall as he said, "The kind you're best at, of course. None of the confidence men or even their company guards wanted to be anywhere near that old charcoal burner when he was found dead. So you made sure he'd be found dead at a time anyone he'd ever sold a lick of charcoal to had an alibi. That even fooled old Dutch Steinmuller. He couldn't figure out what was going on. He only knew *something* was up. Then he discovered the mine shaft he'd kept reporting as pumped dry was suddenly filled with

water again. That was the magic missing word: *again*. He
sent a hasty wire. Strapped for eating money after all he'd
wasted on postage to no avail, he tried to save a nickel by
leaving out one vital word. It came over the wire as an
urgent message that the Tombstone Lode was flooded, pe-
riod. Nobody paid attention. I'd have never heard about it
at all had not some wire-service relay operator, trying to
make sense out of a meaningless message, took it upon
himself to try to *make* it make some sense. Somebody
spotted Dutchy sending the wire and asked some innocent-
sounding questions, or mayhaps the old man just gossiped
to the wrong barkeep, or mayhaps none of you knew about
that and he just wound up with that rifle ball in him when
one of you caught him snooping about the Lucky Cuss for
further details. I don't reckon any judge or jury will worry
about the motive, once at least one of you is charged with
shooting the poor old cuss, do you?"

Skagway Sam didn't answer just yet. One of his gunslicks growled, "He knows too much and we'll never get a
crack at him any better than this one, boss."

Skagway Sam smiled crookedly across the pool table at
Stringer as he purred, "Nobody will be coming down off
the slopes this side of three, Pecos. I'd sort of like to know
just how much he really knows. How much do you really
know, old son?"

Stringer said, "The law will have to sort out some of the
details. But I reckon I have the general outline drawn to
my satisfaction."

Skagway Sam chuckled, suggesting, "Draw it more to
my own satisfaction, MacKail. All this time, I been thinking we was pals. If we ain't pals, who in blue blazes has
been gunning for *both* of us since first we met?"

Stringer shook his head. "Nice try. I surely would have let that border Mex badman gun you in the Tucson yards had I known then what I know now. But I didn't. So when Jesus Garcia tried to pay you back for killing old Morales, who could have been kin for all I know, I acted the fool and only did what came natural. Lucky for me, Garcia was a wanted man. You sent a she-male confederate back in hopes of finding out what on earth could be going on. I thought I got into Miss Tillie sort of easy, but I reckon I owe you and Miss Faro Fran for a pleasant layover in Tucson. Once she'd sort of gotten to know me better, she wired on ahead that I was about as dumb and harmless as you hoped I might be.

"Your boy, Knuckles, started up with me on his own. We can both agree he was simply a stupid bully boy, of no use to you or me. Our big dramatic scene out on the street that time gave you a no-lose grandstand play. Knuckles didn't know he was on his own until even he could figure he was. Had he killed me in front of God and everybody, they'd have arrested him, you and the others would have just seemed surprised, and I'd have been out of your way. When Knuckles backed down once more it gave you the chance to declare your undying love for me. Then you sent Knuckles after me again, giving him one last chance to prove himself, and when that didn't work, you got rid of him as useless. I'm still trying to figure out whether it was you or Faro Fran who decided to blow me up, more than once."

Skagway Sam smiled expansively and said, "Oh, that was my own notion, old son. Old Fran kept saying there was no sense killing you if you didn't know nothing. I figured that sooner or later you'd find out something and, as we can all see, you sure went and did, you nosy cuss."

"That bushy-browed pal who wired a warning about me while you and Faro Fran were over in L.A. must have told you I was good, eh?"

The burly tinhorn replied, "He warned us you was the best, and that you'd exposed salted-mine schemes before. By the way, we ain't seen old Klondike since we sent him after you last night. Would you like to tell us anything about that, seeing these would seem to be your last words in any case?"

Stringer said, "I'm not sure. Would this Klondike with the bushy eyebrows be the gent who's so free with dynamite bombs?"

Skagway Sam nodded jovially. "He sure would. You must have more damn lives than a cat. But I reckon we've about run out of things to say, don't you?"

Stringer didn't answer with words. At four-to-one odds there was only one sensible answer, so he drew and fired as he crabbed sideways with his back to the wall. His first shot took Skagway Sam in the groin, blowing off one ball and dropping him to the floor, bawling in pure agony. Even before he got there, Stringer had shot the one called Pecos in the mouth, snapping off his front teeth but curing his toothache, before it could start, by severing his brain stem. Then the space where Stringer had been sliding along the wall was pockmarked by hot lead, and powdered plaster drifted amid the gunsmoke. Meanwhile he'd taken a head-first dive under the pool table, landed on one shoulder, and kept rolling to wind up at the feet of the two gunslicks on the far side.

Since they were still peering across the table into the gunsmoke where he might have been, Stringer's two shots raked up into their guts, and they went down as well.

That left Stringer with exactly one round in the wheel. Skagway Sam was rolling all over the messy floor, bawling for his mother, a doctor, and at least a dozen saints. Stringer growled, "Aw, shut up," and silenced him forever with his last shot.

Then he sat up, ears ringing and belly filled with butter-flies, and began to reload as Wes Rhodes dashed in, his own gun drawn, to gasp, "Stringer, did you make it?" Then the lawman peered deeper into the blue haze to add, "Jesus H. Christ, I see you did, you murderous bundle of bobcats! What in the hell do they feed growing boys in Calaveras County, anyways?"

Stringer got to his feet—it wasn't easy—and hung on to the pool table with one hand as he holstered his gun with the other and asked, "Did you hear Skagway Sam admit to enough guilty knowledge to justify my suicide attempt?"

Rhodes pointed his chin at the small window opened a crack, above the six or eight bullet holes in the rear wall, as he replied, "I did. So did the two deputies with me. I got 'em covering us out front and back, just in case you failed to wipe out the gang entire. What got into you just now, Stringer? We kept waiting and waiting for you to give the password to move in. The next thing we knowed all hell was busting loose in here! Didn't your mother never warn you how dumb it was for one man to take on four in a stand-up shoot-out?"

Deciding he might not puke, after all, Stringer let go of the table and told the lawman, "That's why I wasn't stand-ing up near the end. The original plan, as you may recall, was for me to question Skagway Sam lonesome. I wasn't expecting those others to butt in and, when they did, I hadn't tricked their boss into admitting all that much."

"You still should have signaled to move in," said Rhodes.

"To what end?" Stringer asked. "You couldn't have held them on anything. There's no law against watching a gent shoot eight ball in a public pool hall. I was about to signal you when Skagway Sam figured *he'd* heard enough, as well. After that there just wasn't time to do anything but what I had to."

Wes Rhodes grimaced down at the bodies sprawled across the blood-spattered floor. "You sure done it. I don't hear the usual thundering herd coming this way. I reckon you must have just cleaned the plows of all the brave ones in the bunch and I know for a fact that most of the town, innocent or guilty, is up by the Lucky Cuss right now."

He hauled out his pocket watch, consulted it, and said, "The sheriff's posse we sent for figures to get here from Bisbee sooner or later. I don't see how they'll ever make it before them other crooks blast the salted face and start passing out ore samples and worthless mining stock. I can rustle up half a dozen good men to back our play. With these four real killers out of the way, we ought to be able to nip the flimflam in the bud, right?"

"Wrong," said Stringer, soberly. "Such a move would be braver than smart for three reasons. To begin with, we don't know how many in the bunch are real killers. At least one bushy-browed bastard with a crippled gun hand but Lord knows how much dynamite is still running loose, and the company guards up the slope are still an unknown quality. In the second place, it will be after banking hours when they blast, around three P.M."

Rhodes frowned, protesting, "Hell, Stringer, nobody's

likely to ask for a bank loan afore they buy any mining
stock. Them poor unsuspecting dudes came here rich
enough to invest in the mine if it looked like a good invest-
ment!"

"Few if any rich folk carry more hard cash on them than
they can afford to lose," Stringer argued. "They carry
checkbooks. That takes us to my third reason for giving the
con men plenty of rope. It'll be too late to cash one check
here in Tombstone. Most of said checks figure to be drawn
on California banks to begin with. I'm betting the crooks
really running the operation will grab that same special
train, checks and all, to cash 'em in L.A. Then they mean
to split up with their swag, long before their dupes here in
Tombstone know they've been left holding the bag."

Rhodes whistled. "They sure must be dirty crooks—
even for crooks, I mean."

"Confidence men are betrayers by profession," Stringer
declared. "The longer their dupes here stay in operation,
the farther away the ringleaders mean to be with the money
when it finally sinks in that they sold a soggy hole in the
ground."

Smiling boyishly, Rhodes said, "It's a good thing we're
on to them, then. So when do I get to arrest 'em if you
want me to give 'em some slack?"

Stringer said, "You don't have to. Once they cross a
state line with their loot it gets to be a federal case. I sug-
gest you wire the U.S. marshal's office in L.A. They're
not far from the Union Depot, and they'll know what to do
when that special rolls in a few days from now. The freshly
stung witnesses they'll need to convict the bastards will be
aboard the same train, see?"

Rhodes did. He was paid to be a smart lawman. But he

still looked sort of wistful as he said, "Shit, you ain't no fun at all, Stringer. Me and my boys was hoping to share *some* of the credit, at least."

Stringer grimaced down at the body of Skagway Sam. "You can have these four killers, if you want all the paper-work that goes with killing even a killer. We know Knuckles Ashton was wanted in other parts and he was the *sissy* of the bunch."

Rhodes studied silently for a time. He was fairly honest, as well as pragmatic. Then, as Stringer hoped, practical considerations about rewards and reps won out. "It's sure lucky for you that once I heard Skagway Sam say all them mean things about himself I come in that front door just in time to save you, right?" he said, grinning wickedly.

"That's about the size of it. But you'd better cut your deputies in on it if you want to keep it a family matter," Stringer declared, a matching grin on his face.

"I would have, anyways. Both the boys are kissing kin. I'd best send one to scout up some help with all these cadavers afore they commence to stink. This afternoon fig-ures to get hotter afore it gets cooler. What am I supposed to tell that posse from Bisbee when it shows up? They're likely to feel mighty chagrined if I tell 'em they rid all that way on a fool's errand."

Stringer agreed, "They'll have some work cut out for them when they ride in. I figure they ought to make it this side of sundown if I know anything about maps and ponies. They'll get here somewhat tuckered from a half-day's riding in this kind of weather. So we'd best rest and water 'em in, say, the Crystal Palace as we hold a war conference with 'em."

Rhodes said, "That ought to soothe 'em, some. But the

railroad dispatcher tells me that special is pulling out for parts west, just around sundown. Won't that be cutting our war plans thin, whatever the hell they are?"

"No. The timing should be just right. We won't want the sheriff's men moving in to arrest all the rascals around the Lucky Cuss until after that trainload of dudes and the ringleaders pulls out. Exposing the flimflam while the flimflammed suckers are still here could cause a lot of confusion and the crooks could get rid of the evidence amid all the tears and recriminations. They have to be nailed by federal marshals with the goods on 'em, after crossing at least one state line, unless you'd rather see a local county trial drag on for years. But if you and your own town lawmen feel really busy, you might want to make an arrest or two on purely local matters before the curtain goes up for the bigger show."

Asked what he meant by purely local matters, Stringer explained, "The hotshots running the mining-stock swindle were too slick to dirty their own hands with local blood. They hired Skagway Sam and Faro Fran to deal with any killing that was called for. I have reason to believe it was Faro Fran who really called the shots. As you can plainly see, old Skagway was little more than a mean bully boy. The gal struck me as a heap smarter. She reined him in when he got tough just for the hell of it. But that means she gave final approval when her boys really got around to someone she thought it wise to kill. So the murder of old Dutch Steinmuller, likely the mysterious death of Morales, the charcoal burner, and the murder of Miss Iona Fraser with a dynamite bomb meant for me can be attributed to Miss Faro Fran, directly."

Wes Rhodes growled, "Cochise County will be proud to

contribute a rope to hang such a murdersome bitch. She and her whores ought to be up at the Lucky Cuss right now, too!"

Shaking his head, Stringer said, "I thought you were paying attention out back. Skagway Sam's backup *told* him they'd been sent by Faro Fran. Her whores may be up there by the mine, but she was down here, minding the store. By now she'll be packing, unless she's deaf. She can't hope to hide out here in town. So what'll you bet she and Klondike will want to board that sunset train with the others?"

Everything went about as planned until it was pushing sunset, the locomotive bell was clanging its intentions to back down the spur track, and neither Faro Fran nor the murderous Klondike had seen fit to show up at trackside as yet.

Stringer and Wes Rhodes had posted themselves near the cab of the engine so that everyone moving down the platform to board had to pass them. Some town and county deputies were strung out to cover every boarding point, armed not only with their guns but detailed descriptions of the two wanteds. But while a heap of mighty odd-looking dudes had boarded the special so far, not a one had been a bushy-browed gent with his right wing in a sling or the flashy Faro Fran almost everyone from Tombstone knew on sight.

Stringer looked up from the smoke he was rolling when he heard a she-male voice call him a bastard. It was good old W. R. Hackman of the L.A. *Examiner*. The petite blonde was lugging a light valise until she put it down near Stringer and told him, "Your stuff is behind the lobby counter at the hotel, you doublecrossing bastard. I thought you told me you'd share the story if I kept it for you."

He smiled sheepishly. "The story's not over yet. I wasn't out to double-cross you, ma'am. I have to change trains in L.A. on my way home. I'd be proud to buy you a Coca-Cola and let you in on what I know, once I know it."

She stamped her foot and pouted, "Don't lie to me, damm it. I didn't even see you in the crowd when they made that strike up at the Lucky Cuss this afternoon. Do you call that sharing a story?"

Wes Rhodes looked uncomfortable and drifted on down the platform to let them sort things out. The perky blonde was warming up to the subject as she added, "Then, when I got back to the hotel this afternoon they told me there'd been a big gun battle just down the street and that you'd been in it or surely watching it. But did you offer me one eyewitness paragraph? You did not. I had to patch it together as best I could from a dozen different versions!"

"If I could get a word in edgeways, ma'am," Stringer pleaded. "You weren't at the Cosmopolitan when I looked for you there, more than once. I haven't been trying to hide anything from you. I've been busy as a one armed paperhanger in a wind storm. If you really want a story, a big one, be advised to march right back to the hotel and wait for me there. I promise I'll share the scoop with you as soon as I've time to sit down, okay?"

She looked up at him uncertainly, thought about that, and then she set her little jaw more firmly. "Oh, sure you will," she said. "You must think I'm a real country girl. You're trying to make me miss this train so that you can even scoop me on the little I've found out on my own!"

He assured her, "I wasn't planning on boarding this train. I only came down to see some folk off. I can't leave Tombstone for at least a day or so. Both the county coroner and county grand jury want me to fill out some depositions before I leave. I mean to wire my final report in, anyway. My own paper would never forgive me if we were scooped while I was making my way home by rail, even if I was free to leave this instant. So, no fooling, W. R., you'd better stick around. Things may be happening, here, long before you can make it home to L.A., and I'm sure Western Union will give you the same special rates on news dispatches."

She hesitated, wrinkled her perky nose at him, and decided, "You must not know any women here in Tombstone. I think you're pretty, too, but no thanks. I'm a newspaperwoman, not a playtoy, if it's all the same to you!" Then she picked up her valise and marched on, her nose in the air and, damm it, her rear view just plain teasing, whether she was walking that way on purpose or not.

Stringer watched her fade out of his life in the gathering gloom of twilight. Then he shrugged, lit the smoke he'd been rolling all the time, and turned absently to see how many more passengers might be coming. He knew they'd better be coming fast if they meant to make the train. The bell had stopped clanging. The crew up in the cab was just waiting for the conductor's signal to open the throttle. Stringer saw a slightly taller but less teasy-walking female figure coming his way with a carpetbag in each hand and her straw boater cocked at an awkward angle atop her Gibson Girl hairdo. As she spotted him, she faltered in midstride, then kept coming, a resigned little smile on her pale face. He ticked his hat brim to her and said, "Evening, Miss Tillie. Your hat's coming unpinned. I've been wondering where you went, after Tucson."

She stopped, put down her bags, and said, "So, now you know."

He shook his head. "Not hardly. You told me in Tucson you were bound here to work as a librarian. It took me a spell to figure out you were one of Faro Fran's gals, and for that I thank you. I'd have never enjoyed our first meeting in Tucson if I'd known, then, how you'd learned to screw so fine."

She looked hurt as she said, "All right, I'm a whore. I wouldn't expect you to understand. Let's say it just happened. I still meant some of the things I said, in bed, long ago and far away."

He said, "I'm glad. It makes me feel less dumb about the way *I* might have acted in bed. Did Faro Fran say it was time to light out or was this your own idea, Tillie?"

She heaved a defeated little sigh. "I'm not quite sure what that painted hussy and Skagway Sam were really up to. I confess I bought their story that you could be a hired gun when they sent me back to spy on you that time. But it seems that was only *one* of the lies they told us girls. None of us know, for sure, what's been going on. But I, for one, don't mean to go down with the ship."

He didn't answer. She licked her pale lips and asked him, in a timid tone, "Am I free to board, now, honey?"

He said, "I'm still thinking about that. I'm not about to bear witness against you for crimes against nature in Tucson, and the law here has enough bigger fish to fry. But, ah, where did you say old Faro Fran might be holed up, right now?"

Before she could answer, if she intended to answer, another female voice, behind him, screamed, "MacKail! Look out!" Stringer slid sideways into the slot between the locomotive's tender and the mail car as two shots rang out almost as one.

Then it got very quiet. Stringer risked a cautious peek out of his dark slot, gun in hand, to see the whore he'd just been talking to flat on her back between her bags. He saw gunsmoke and heard running footsteps coming at him from the other way. Another dark human form lay facedown under the cloud of smoke as it began to clear. Then W. R. Hackman appeared through the blue haze, her bitty right hand gripping a bitty nickel-plated pocket pistol. She stopped by the body she'd back-shot, sobbing, "He was about to shoot you in the back!"

Stringer muttered, "There seems to be a lot of that going around, this evening." He stared both ways at both bodies, trying to piece the picture together. He holstered his own gun as he joined the petite blonde by the other. He said, "Put that away and let me do the talking," as, sure enough, Wes Rhodes and four other lawmen bore down on them, their own guns drawn.

Stringer called out, "Hold your fire, boys. It's over. This little lady threw down on the results you see at our feet, just as he was set to fire at my back. He fired anyway and nailed the gal yonder, by her baggage. So allow me to present W. R. Hackman, the hero of the hour. Or should I say heroine?"

Wes Rhodes rolled the dead man over with his boot. The light was tricky, but as they all regarded the bushy brows and taped-up right wrist, the town law agreed, "She surely did a heroic job on this mean cuss. He'd be the one as murdered poor Iona Fraser with dynamite, right?"

Stringer nodded and said, "Her, at least. It hardly matters who killed whom, with all of the killers accounted for."

Wes Rhodes allowed that sounded fair and asked who the other victim might be, so Stringer said, "Oh, that's old Faro Fran. You might say her demise was an accident, but I can't say I'm sorry. She was the lethal brains directing Skagway Sam and the others."

Wes Rhodes led the march up the platform to where the dead gal lay, staring up at the purple sky with an innocent little smile on her pale lips.

Rhodes hunkered over her, shook his head, and said, "No offense, Stringer, but this gal don't look at all like Faro Fran!"

Stringer said, "She fooled me, too, for a spell. But when you get down to cases, how were any of us supposed to know what the one and original Faro Fran really looked like under that red wig and all that face paint? When she was being Faro Fran she talked different and acted different. It was easy enough for her to turn into another gal entire when she wanted to, or had to."

W. R. Hackman was recovering from her shock and recalling she was a newspaperwoman by now. So it was her idea to ask Stringer how on earth he'd recognized the pathetic drab at their feet as the wicked woman of Tombstone.

He said, "To begin with, she and her gang never would have come to Tombstone if they hadn't been offered a handsome cut by the mining stock swindlers. I'm sorry, Wes, but facts are facts. I didn't recognize her as two gals I'd—ah—met up with on separate occasions until just before her confederate tried to shoot me in the back while she was distracting me so demurely. Let's say there's simply limits to how dumb one man can be about womankind. Her story was making no sense and so, as I was trying to figure out what she was really up to, I was naturally thinking back and forth betwixt Faro Fran and less gussied-up gals who had to be in with the gang. I couldn't see Miss Tillie working as one of Faro Fran's gals with not a trace of makeup or perfume, so I pictured mousy Tillie with powder and paint all over her innocent face and it came to me who she was just as her new boyfriend was throwing down at me. He couldn't hear us talking. She'd have no doubt preferred he hold his fire and let her bluff her way through. But she once told me she found good help hard to find, and so that's about the whole story."

Little W. R. said, "The heck you say. I have to get it on paper and then the wire, fast!"

Wes Rhodes straightened up and shook his head at her, not unkindly, as he told her, "I fear you won't be going nowheres until you explain these two dead bodies to the satisfaction of this county, ma'am."

At her dismayed look, Stringer quickly assured her, "I'll be proud to bear witness for you and, as I said before, we can both wire the story in from here, see?"

"I'm beginning to." She sighed. "How long do you think we'll both be stuck here in Tombstone, MacKail?"

He said, "Oh, no more than a week. I'd best get your valise and escort you back to the hotel. The boys will tidy up here, for now. Is that jake with you, Wes?"

With a knowing smile, Wes said, "Sure, you young folk run along. No doubt you have a lot to talk about."

As Stringer led her away from the crowd encircling the bodies, the train was backing out as well. Her valise stood, lonesome, where she'd dropped it to save his life. Picking it up, he told her, "It was lucky for me you were still on the platform when that rascal threw down on me from behind. How come you hadn't boarded yet?"

She fluttered her lashes as she answered, shyly, "I was on my way back to take you up on your offer. Last night I took the liberty of reading the copy you left in my safe-keeping. You're a hell of a writer, MacKail. If we put our heads together on this scoop we ought to come up with a humdinger!"

Taking her arm in his free hand, he said he sure hoped so. As they headed back to the Cosmopolitan Hotel and only Dan Cupid knew what else, she must have felt obliged to proclaim, "I hope you understand that when I said I wanted to work with you, that's all I had in mind."

He just smiled and squeezed her arm. It might have sounded a mite fresh if he'd pointed out, so soon, that a lady always had a right to change her mind. The evening was young and with any luck the two of them would have their heads together quite a spell.